"WE'LL TAKE THAT GUN..."

Slocum drew the Colt carefully out of its holster. "But I'm aiming to stop in on Miles," he said suddenly, without handing the gun over. "You boys work for Miles?"

"What do you want with him?"

"My business."

Two of the men had dropped their guns back into their holsters, and only the speaker was covering Slocum.

"Kane, he don't look like anybody Miles wants to see," said the smallest of the three.

Kane, a big man with a big beard, let the hammer down on his cylinder, carefully, slowly.

"What do you think, Joey?" he said.

Joey, a man with a patch over his eye, spat over the side of his leg. "What do you think, Dutch?"

Dutch, a squat man with short legs, but a long trunk, sniffed. "He is too damn smart for my money, boys. Let's string him up."

OTHER BOOKS BY JAKE LOGAN

JAKE LOGAN

SLOCUM AND THE CATTLE WAR

BERKLEY BOOKS, NEW YORK

SLOCUM AND THE CATTLE WAR

A Berkley Book/published by arrangement with
the author

PRINTING HISTORY
Berkley edition/January 1990

ISBN: 0-425-11919-X

A BERKLEY BOOK ® TM 757,375
Berkley Books are published by The Berkley Publishing Group,
200 Madison Avenue, New York, New York 10016.
The name "BERKLEY" and the "B" logo
are trademarks belonging to Berkley Publishing Corporation.

PRINTED IN THE UNITED STATES OF AMERICA

10   9   8   7   6   5   4   3   2   1

1

Slocum knew the scene. Any western town on the Fourth of July was more than likely to put on a shooting match, with the usual motley bunch of contestants. And Medicine Butte was no exception. The big, broad-shouldered man with raven-black hair, green eyes, and a casual yet wholly alert manner stood away from the crowd gathered near the empty cattle pens at one end of town and regarded the participants.

They were the customary collection of out-of-work holdup men who had just been hanging around until the next excitement came their way, a gent who looked like a lawman, though he had no tin showing, a couple of cowboys, two drunks, plus the usual handful of drifters looking for a chance to pick up a few easy dollars.

"Gonna try your hand, stranger?"

1

The raspy voice came from behind him, and Slocum knew it was directed at him. He waited a moment before acknowledging the presence of the man he'd spotted a couple of moments ago.

"Good way to pick up a few dollars an' have fun besides," the voice went on. "Those fellers look like they ain't about to hit the side of a barn with a cannon."

Slocum moved his head then, though without changing his stance, as the speaker came into view, stepping nimbly around his left side. "Sometimes a man can surprise you," Slocum said easily, just to be conversational. "Especially when it's guns."

The other man spat briefly in the direction of the two men who were lining up the names of the contestants. He was of medium height, and bony all over, with a lined face and a thick, drooping mustache under a long nose. His agate-colored eyes gleamed. Their lids were thick, heavy, folded into deep sockets. Slocum took in a lazy quickness in his canted head, pursed lips, and the impression he gave of a predator. He seemed all eyes, elbows, and knees.

For a moment Slocum wondered if he was talking to the law, even though there was no sign of a badge on the other man's clothing. Then he decided not.

"That saloon yonder is a good one," the man said now, nodding past Slocum. "The Buffalo Bar. I oughta know; I own it." He released a humorless chuckle.

"Drop over if you've a mind to. I mean when you get dry."

Slocum nodded. "Might." And he caught something extra in the other man's eyes—it was there for just a split second, then was swiftly covered by a sleek smile and a nod.

There was something about the man that had put him on his guard. Did he know him? He did look a little familiar. But no. A man like that he'd remember when and where. That type wasn't one you'd forget. Yes, he had a lot of force. Though on the thin side he gave the impression of physical strength and determination. But Slocum didn't want the other man to see that he was sizing him up, so he turned his attention back to the men lining up for the shooting match.

The distance set was twenty paces, the weapons were .45-caliber revolvers, and the prizes ranged from $200 for first down to $100 for second and $50 for third.

There was a lively traffic in side bets. The qualifying round, which was intended to get rid of the amateurs and concentrate the contest on the serious shootists, required that three out of ten bullets hit the bull's-eye. This area was about the size of a silver dollar, though at twenty paces it looked—as some lively contestant put it—"no bigger'n an asshole on a drunk pissant."

By three o'clock in the afternoon all but one of the entrants had taken a shot. Out of the thirty-odd men who had tried only thirteen had qualified.

The last man to step up to the firing line was an insignificant-looking fellow of maybe thirty-five, with a heavy black longhorn mustache that looked like it was pulling his thin face into the many lines that gave it the expression one might have associated with a gravedigger.

He couldn't have weighed more than a hundred and twenty pounds soaking wet, and he stood no higher than the withers on a stubby cow pony. The ends of his trouser legs fell inches short of his clod-hopper boots. Under bib overalls he wore a hickory shirt with a tear at the neckline.

"Sure don't look like much, do he?" the owner of the Buffalo Bar said to the back of John Slocum's head.

At this remark, Slocum turned and looked fully at the man who for some reason had decided to again converse with him. "I'd say it was a question of who can hit the bull's-eye there, less than whether he looks like he ate grizzly for breakfast."

But the crowd evidently didn't agree with Slocum. There were not a few snickers when the contestant cocked an old, scarred .45 with a chewed-up hand grip and leveled it on the target. A roar of laughter broke from the crowd when the first shot missed the target completely, kicking up dirt on one side.

But the little man was undismayed, and, taking a long breath, he drew down once more on the target. This time the scorekeeper signaled a near miss. The bullet had split the ring separating the eight–nine circle.

"Hell, the man's just gettin' hisself loosed up," somebody said, and this was greeted with another round of sneering laughter.

The third shot was still outside the bull's-eye, but the fourth cut the black. The fifth bullet was low, down in the number-three circle, and it didn't look like the little man had much of a chance.

But Slocum wasn't convinced. He could tell by the way the skinny man handled the pistol that somebody was going to be making a lot of money. And it was no surprise to him when a man standing at the edge of the crowd—obviously a stranger in town—offered to bet $50 that the shooter would qualify, and he was beset by a number of takers.

Slocum almost let his grin show when he saw how the betting appeared to unnerve the shooter even more. His gun muzzle began to waver all over the target, and he had to lower the piece and aim it again. The shot was three inches high.

Now there were only four shots left, and two of them had to be bull's-eyes for him to qualify. While the shooter reloaded, the man who had bet the $50 that he would qualify was besieged with offers of further bets.

"Two to one he don't make it!" someone shouted, and waved bills in the air. "Gents, that's two hundred to one! Who's taking? Who's taking!"

"I'll take that," the stranger said calmly, and drew a cigar from his breast pocket.

Slocum took note of the fine quality of his clothes. And suddenly—there it was. Lighting his cigar, his eyes moved to look at the man standing beside Slocum. It was in the flash of a second, but it clicked with something inside Slocum.

But at this point the contestant had turned and looked at the noisy crowd in silent appeal. It was as though he was asking their help.

He said nothing, but the manager of the shooting

match shouted, "Give him a chance! He's paid his entry fee like everybody else!"

The seventh shot was a bull's-eye, and the astonished onlookers cheered loudly. The eighth and ninth shots were down in the number-two circle, and the crowd was silent. When his last shot hit the bull's-eye the crowd broke into a great cheer.

"Not much to show, I'd allow," the man standing near Slocum said.

But Slocum had seen the look on the face of the man who had been taking bets, had felt the contact between him and the man who had just spoken. "He made it," Slocum pointed out.

"You puttin' money on that?" the saloonkeeper said agreeably.

"Nope."

Though the crowd had cheered the little man with the big gun, no one deigned to bet on his chances now that he was up against the others who had qualified; they had all made a better showing.

Because he was the last to qualify, the short man came up for his turn at the tail end of the match with some pretty stiff scores staring at him. Two shooters —a local bigmouth named Hansen and a gray-faced stranger named Helms—were tied with nine bull's-eyes and the tenth bullet in the number-nine ring—as close as anyone could come without scoring ten straight bull's-eyes. Six others had eight bull's-eyes each for second money.

It was evident to Slocum that it was only a sort of inertia, and possibly a small amount of courtesy, that the crowd remained for the final contestant to take his turn. Everyone was looking toward the close shoot-off between the two top men and paid small attention to the man in the torn hickory shirt and bib overalls as he drew his battered .45 from its cutaway holster, looked at the target a moment, then drew down on it.

What followed took the crowd completely by surprise. Without lowering his gun between shots, the little man with the big mustache blasted out six bullets, with only a brief pause between each shot as the gun was recocked and quickly aimed.

The flabbergasted scorekeeper signaled six bull's-eyes, but the crowd was too stunned by what was happening to raise more than a moderate cheer.

Slocum told himself that by now the bettors had to know that they'd been taken. Obviously they were too astonished to protest.

Meanwhile, to Slocum's amusement, the saloonkeeper, still standing near him, let out a great sigh. "Well, by God, there goes my bet."

It was then he realized who the saloonkeeper really was. Whatever it was that had been plucking at him about the man had surely been right. Slocum wondered what name he was currently using. Well, he would see when the moment came.

By now the thin man with the sad-looking face and the big black mustache had slipped four more cartridges into the cylinder of his .45. The crowd waited with mild interest as he raised his arm and fired the four rounds one right after the other.

As the sound of the final shot died away, the scorekeeper waved his arms in the air with all ten fingers spread. "Jumpin' J. H. Christ!" he shouted. "Ten bull's-eyes!"

"A great way to celebrate the Fourth of July, wouldn't you say, stranger?"

Slocum looked at the saloonkeeper. "I congratulate you," he said with just the hint of a smile on his face.

The other man took it easily. "The name is Ratigan, Mr. Slocum. Ulysses Ratigan." He smiled broadly, as if sharing a joke. "It *is* the famous John Slocum I be talkin' to, no less?"

"I do believe I'll take you up on that drink," Slocum said by way of reply.

"Glad to hear that, sir."

"I expect the winner yonder will head for your saloon with all of them that's still cheering him."

"I'll wager he won't be wanting nothing he can't get this night. But of course the people of Medicine Butte are free to go where they like, and it might not be where I'm located. There's plenty of good drinkin' places in this here town."

"I'll bet on them going to yours," Slocum said with a quiet grin. And he looked right into the other man's agate-colored eyes.

Ratigan cleared his throat. "There are certain aspects about you, Mr. Slocum—and I mean no offense, these are interesting aspects, though a man might find some of them troublesome. One of them is that you mince no words. However..." He cleared his throat again, heavily this time, and spat vigorously at the ground. It lay there, a glob of tobacco juice, spittle, and phlegm, shining a little in the brilliant sunlight. "However, I'll look for you in the Buffalo." He turned then and without another word walked off in the direction of the center of town.

In the meantime the suddenly famous shootist had collected his winnings, as had the stranger who had been swamped with bets from the locals. But the stranger had vanished, though Slocum had a strong feeling he would see the gentleman again. While the hero of the hour—the little man with the big .45— was being carried to the nearest saloon—which just happened to be the Buffalo Bar.

Slocum, following after, was grinning to himself as he saw how everything had turned out according to tradition. There was certainly no denying it: Shiner Ratigan was one of the great bunco artists. And John Slocum was looking forward to hanging around Medicine Butte to see what was going to happen next.

Now, making his way toward the Buffalo Bar, he was also remembering his adventure up on Elbow Creek only the day before, when he'd been shot out of his saddle, landing on his already wounded arm. It had been close. And in a certain way it had been worth it.

2

The breakup had come early that year. Before a man could scratch himself the big snows were melting in the mountains and the rivers—chock-full of ice, dead trees, and other debris—were roaring down from the high country. The Lazy Water was no exception, running over its banks as it rushed through the long valley and on to the south country.

Slocum hadn't been in the Lazy Water country in a good while, and he was happy to return. He'd taken lead in a freak gun confrontation at the Willow Creek stage depot—nothing serious, but his arm was still somewhat sore. He was figuring on a rest; it was spring now, and hunting would be more like it. And maybe some cowpunching. He liked working cattle. And he sure liked the Lazy Water country, with its snowcapped mountains, its sweeping valleys, and always the great, limitless sky, which seemed bigger than anywhere else.

In the late forenoon he had topped the high ridge and drew rein in the shadow of a stand of spruce. He sat his spotted pony there in the silence of the big shadow that covered him and his horse, his eyes searching beyond to the sky cut like metal over the tremendous mountain peaks, which were capped with snow that would remain all summer long.

And suddenly catching the glint of sunlight on metal he was out of the stock saddle as the bullet spanged off rock and went singing into the depths of the great valley. And he was rolling over sagebrush and rocks, over the edge of the draw, at last pulling up hard behind a thick pine tree.

He had the big Navy Colt in his hand. Behind the pine, with his face pressed to the hard ground, he waited in glaring sunlight. He lay absolutely still, listening.

In the sky above, nothing moved. He heard the trees stirring. His pony had spooked and now stood waiting several feet away from where Slocum lay, his ears up as he looked about carefully, snorting a little, but not even thinking of feeding on the lush grass that lay near his feet. Slocum kept an eye on the animal as he tried to locate the source of the gunshot, watching the pony's reactions, relying on him to let him know when danger came.

He waited, sinking as much as he could into the pine needles on top of the hard ground. His hearing was better now as his body quieted. But he had fallen on his sore arm, and it was throbbing. Still, he could pull a trigger, and he also knew how to shoot with his left hand. He watched his pony's ears, reading the situation from the way those ears moved.

Who could have shot at him? He was sure no one had cut his trail, for he'd checked it carefully and often. No, he was certain he hadn't been followed. Whoever had fired that shot had to be from right around here. Still, it was not so much a question of who, but where. Where was the bugger?

He waited, his ear right on the ground, breathing the odor of pine, sage, his pony, with the heat of the high sun drilling into his back.

Suddenly, from the side of his vision, he saw a jay fly up from a clump of young pine. He would have given plenty for his rifle, but there'd been no chance to pull the Winchester free of its scabbard as he'd spilled out of his saddle.

He turned his head slowly to see if he could catch the movement of the man in that stand of pine. And all at once another shot rang out and the spotted pony screamed as the bullet creased its rump.

Slocum stayed down, allowing only a single cussword to form silently on his lips. For at that distance, and with no solid view of the bushwhacker, he couldn't risk a shot with the Colt.

The sun was straight up when at last he saw a branch move at the same time as his ears caught the crackle and swish of underbrush. A short man, wearing a mackinaw too big for him, stepped out of the timber, apparently satisfied that it was perfectly safe. He had to be a damned fool, Slocum told himself. His face was not yet visible, and he appeared hesitant. He was holding a Henry rifle with a worn stock.

Slocum measured the distance. He had to be sure. If his arm hadn't been so sore he could have taken the chance and shot at him. Only now the arm wasn't only sore, it was numb.

And so he waited—until the man with the Henry suddenly turned and he could see his face. And it was a young girl! She was wearing a cap with a large peak, and she wore it straight on top of her head, which was covered with a great spilling of corn-yellow hair. A kid!

Still, he had waited. This was no time to let his surprise cost him his caution. It could easily be a trap, with someone covering the girl from the timber of those rocks over yonder.

But John Slocum was a patient man; he knew the value of patience. Besides, there was no need for him to move. It was up to the drygulcher to discover whether he was alive or dead. It was his—rather, her—move.

And so Slocum waited. All he had right now was his patience, and he didn't aim to give it away.

The girl looked over at the pony, who was looking at her, then she looked carefully around the line of timber, her eyes moving over the place where Slocum was hidden.

Finally, evidently seeing nothing, the girl turned, and now she had her back to Slocum.

Slocum waited a beat, then raised himself carefully. "Don't move!" he said to the back of that big mackinaw. He watched the girl's shoulders tighten, and now he stepped from behind the pine tree. "Drop the Henry."

The rifle fell at the girl's feet.

"The gunbelt."

He could tell her hands were shaking even though he couldn't see them, as she unbuckled her gunbelt and let it fall.

"Walk four steps forward and stay."

When she had done so, Slocum moved forward quickly, without a sound, and picked up the Henry and the gunbelt. He studied the sun for a moment, then said, "Take three more steps and turn around."

The girl did so, and when she turned to face him the sun was right in her eyes, as Slocum had known it would be. And she was also on lower ground than he.

She was young, maybe thirteen; and she was scared. Plenty scared, Slocum could see. Yet he could see too that she was holding on to herself.

Slocum drew back the hammer of the Colt and saw the tightening of the girl's whole body, while her face paled. But she kept her wide eyes right on him.

"You alone?"

She started to speak, but nodded instead.

"Where's your horse?"

"Back home."

"Where's home?"

He saw her bite her lip then.

"Young lady, you came close to shooting not only my horse but me. And I don't favor that kind of thing. I'm a stranger in this part of the country, so the least you can do is be hospitable."

"I didn't mean to hit your horse. You're on our land. I was only trying to scare you off."

"You are some helluva shot, miss."

The girl said nothing to that. She shifted around a

bit on her feet. She was slight, hardly formed yet, but good-looking, with wide-set blue eyes and a generous mouth. She started to put her hands in her pockets then, but didn't. Then she said again, "You're on our land. We want you to get off. My sister told Mr. Miles—"

"Miles?"

The girl looked puzzled. "Don't you ride for Mr. Miles?"

"Never heard of the gent." Slocum lowered the hammer back on the Colt and holstered it. "Young lady, you've got guts; either that or you're plumb dumb."

The girl's smooth cheeks reddened. "Huh," she said. "Huh."

"I could've shot you right out of that clump of pine. You make more noise than a cavvy of spooked horses. How come you've lived so long?"

But the girl, though nervous, and scared too, was dead serious. "Then . . . then how come you didn't?"

"What's your name, miss?" Slocum asked, ignoring her question.

"Caney Rourke."

Slocum nodded. "Good enough. My name is Slocum." He started toward his horse. "You can pick up your rifle there. I want to see the damage." He had turned his back to her and was now running his hand over the spotted pony's rump.

"Only a crease. Lucky." He turned toward her. She had picked up her rifle and gunbelt. "You got feed?"

"Yes, we do."

"Lead the way, then. But first, who is there at your place?"

"Only me and my sister Nellie."

He saw her bite her lip then as she realized she'd been giving away too much.

"Miss, I'm only interested in getting some feed for my horse, and maybe a cup of coffee for myself. So there's no need to be scared."

He knew the moment he said it that it was the wrong word. The color rose furiously to her cheeks.

"I am not afraid of you, mister, nor of any of you Rocking Box riders!" And then she bit her lip again. "Well, I mean—anyone. I—well, you can have some feed and coffee."

"I'm game to pay for it," he said.

"Maybe cut up some firewood," she said, and then she clamped her mouth shut, while he felt like grinning but didn't.

It had turned out that Nellie Rourke was not yet back from a neighbor's ranch where she'd gone for some supplies, but Caney had loosened some by the time he'd rubbed down his pony and grained and watered him.

Their place was high up, under the rimrocks, and was impossible to see from below, or indeed from any other direction. An excellent feature, Slocum noted, was that you could see a rider coming for miles, while to the rear the high rimrocks offered further inaccessibility.

Besides the log cabin, there was a small bunkhouse, a round horse corral, and a barn with a room in which someone had a workshop. Slocum noted it in passing as he took care of his horse. There was a saddle horse in the corral, a little bay who looked like he'd been well taken care of. That pleased him. He hadn't asked the girl any questions about any other family members besides her sister. She had told him where Nellie had gone, and that she expected her back soon. Looking down toward the river he saw cattle grazing and wondered if they were part of the Rourke spread.

He forked hay for the spotted pony, and then took a further look around the place. They were mostly surrounded by timber—pine, fir, and spruce. He saw a lot of horse tracks, from what appeared to be a couple of horses. One showed a loose shoe, and when he looked closer at the bay in the corral, he saw it was his right foreleg.

The woodpile was in back of the barn, and so he decided to give his arm a try. It was all right for a few swings, but then it began to hurt and he had to stop. When he heard the girl come up behind him he stuck the ax into a log and turned.

"You've got a game arm," she said, her blue eyes large.

"So I do. But I thought I might be good for some firewood."

"We don't need it that bad, and anyway, the coffee is ready."

He followed her up to the cabin. It consisted of a kitchen, a living room, and, it seemed, two bedrooms.

"What happened to your arm? Is it all right to ask?" she added quickly.

"I got shot. Not bad, though."

"But that wasn't by me!"

"An accident. A few hours ago," he said.

"You a lawman?"

"Nope."

And when he saw the funny look on her face he said. "I'm not an outlaw, either. Just an ordinary saddle bum."

Suddenly her grin took over her whole face. And Slocum started to laugh. Then they were both laughing.

"I don't know what's so funny," she said.

"Neither do I."

She stood up. "Let me look at your arm. I'll bet it needs a clean dressing."

He didn't resist, but sat silently enjoying himself while she examined the small though painful wound, then washed it and put on a dressing.

"By golly, that feels really good," he said. "I mean, I bet I could swing that ax right now."

"No, you must rest it. My father once . . ." And she stopped, and he saw the tightness come into her face.

They were both silent then, until whatever it was that had come into her at the mention of her father began to recede.

After another moment Slocum said, "Good coffee."

"You want more?"

He held out his mug while she filled it.

"You got shoeing tools?"

"I think so. In the barn. In that room." She cocked her head at him. "Why?"

"Your bay horse has a loose front shoe. I'll either fix it or give him a new one, if you got any."

"Good. That will be real good!" And she was back to where she had been before the mention of her father.

"There's a rider coming," Slocum said then.

"Gee, you got good ears."

"Didn't you hear one of the horses nicker just now?"

"Oh, yeah. Yes, I did." And she caught herself. "I guess I wasn't thinking."

"You live alone out here, you and your sister, you better pay good attention."

Her face was dead serious as she looked at him and nodded. Then she was at the window. "It's Nellie," she said. "Oh, I'm glad to see her."

And so was Slocum glad to see her. Nellie Rourke was not much more than twenty or twenty-one. And where her younger sister was good-looking, Nellie was beautiful. At any rate, that was how John Slocum saw her.

He had followed Caney out of the kitchen and then remained standing there while the girl ran to the corral, where her sister had just stepped down from her sorrel horse. He watched them greet each other, and then they turned toward the little dun packhorse that Nellie had been leading and began untying the panniers that contained the supplies Nellie had picked up at a neighboring ranch.

When he started down to the corral and barn, the older girl looked up and smiled at him and then came forward and held out her hand.

He had waited an appropriate amount of time while the girls greeted each other, and had also allowed a moment for Caney to tell her sister what had happened.

Now, as Nellie shook hands with him, he felt something go through him.

"Caney told me how she, uh, ran into you, Mr. Slocum. I'm sorry to hear about that, but I'm glad that the misunderstanding was cleared up."

And he stood there taking in her fresh, clean, almost laughing smile—her youth and beauty—as he offered to help with the panniers.

"But you can't carry with your wound," said Caney severely, and almost pulled the pannier away from him. "I'll take it."

"I can handle it," Slocum said, realizing with a sudden alarm that the girl was jealous. At the same time, it made him feel good.

Nellie was obviously everything her younger sister was one day going to be. And as far as Slocum was concerned, Nellie Rourke couldn't possibly be improved upon. Her figure, looking as though it had been poured into her tight trousers, was a delight. Her breasts seemed to be fighting to escape from her dark green and white shirt, while her buttocks, moving through the cabin door ahead of him, brought his erection to its most rigid attention.

Swiftly, and with ease and laughter, the girls unpacked and began preparing supper. Slocum waited a few moments, finishing his coffee, and then excused himself.

The sun was already dropping behind the rimrocks above the ranch, and he could feel the change in the air as, with the sunlight gone, a coolness wrapped itself around the buildings and corral. But there was still enough light for him to pull the shoe on the bay horse and reshoe him.

It was nearly dark when he finished, and he saw Caney coming toward him.

"I thought you were going to rest that arm," she said.

"I did. It was tired of doing nothing, so I gave it a restful change."

"Smarty-pants!"

He liked the way she was flirting with him. But he wished it was her sister instead.

After supper they chatted awhile, then Slocum left them and went up to the bunkhouse, where he threw his duffel.

He lighted the coal-oil lamp with the intention of cleaning his guns, for he planned to ride out early the following morning before the girls were up. Then he started to strip down his Winchester, laying its pieces out on the floor alongside his bedding.

He heard the step outside, and then the knock on the door. Something jumped inside him as he got quickly to his feet and lifted the door latch.

It was both of them.

"Can we talk to you a minute before you go off?" Nellie said.

"You knew I was leaving?"

"Weren't you?"

He nodded.

"Before we were up," Caney said, her words loaded with reproach.

"Wouldn't want to disturb you in the morning," Slocum said, as they settled down on the floor in front of where he'd started to work on his rifle. "I'm an early riser."

"We wanted to ask you to stay here with us," Nellie said. She glanced at her sister. "Just for a spell anyway. We'd try to pay you something. Maybe in beef. I don't know."

"I see you don't have anybody," Slocum said.

Nellie shook her head. Caney said nothing. She was sitting cross-legged, looking down at her hands.

"No parents? No brother?"

It was Nellie who did most of the talking.

"Mom died about the time the trouble got real bad."

"The trouble? You mean with the big stock-growers?" Slocum asked.

"You know about it?" both girls said, almost speaking together.

"Everybody knows about the Buffalo County war."

"One day. . ." Nellie started to say, then stopped, controlling herself, while she touched her younger sister's arm.

"Don't hurry," Slocum said gently.

"Dad was with the small stockmen," said Nellie. "Mom had just taken sick and died the winter before. But Dad was, I guess, one of the leaders, and one day—it was after it was all over, and the ranchers here had won out against the big outfits—I mean, that's how I learned it. And one day some men came and said he was a rustler and they shot him."

"I suppose they called themselves vigilantes," Slocum said softly. He looked over at Caney Rourke, who was sitting stiffly, with her fists clenched, her eyes tightly shut. She seemed to be holding her breath.

"They claimed Dad had stolen some beef, some cattle," Nellie went on, her lower lip trembling. "And they just . . . shot him."

He watched the tears sparkling in her eyes from the light of the coal-oil lamp.

"Then you were left alone, you two," Slocum said.

"Brom . . ." Caney almost whispered the word.

"Brom was here," Nellie said.

"Your brother?"

She nodded. "Two days later the men came back. They said there had been a mistake. That our father wasn't the one." She turned suddenly toward her sister. "Caney. . ."

"I'm all right. Tell it. We said we were gonna tell it. We never told it to anyone, not till now." And somehow, miraculously it seemed to Slocum, her crying stopped and she straightened her shoulders and looked straight at him. Caney's voice was clear now as she spoke.

"Brom was here. 'You're saying it was all a mistake, then?' he said to the leader. There were three of them. And the man said yes, he was sorry, but it had been a mistake." She stopped, pulling herself together again.

"Caney, let me," said Nellie reaching out and touching her sister.

But the girl shook head. "Brom told us just how it was. He said to them, 'Then you made two mistakes, mister. First you murdered my dad. That was your first mistake. Your second mistake was admitting it to me.' And he killed the three of them."

An appalling silence had fallen into the cabin as she told her story. She had related it as though it was a recital, something memorized for an occasion, a kind of litany.

There was a soft silence then. And in a strange way Slocum felt lighter, swept by something clean. It was almost as if something had opened in him. He had the impulse to reach out and touch one of them —an arm, a hand. Instead, he said, "And that was after the war was over, after everything had been settled."

"Yes," Nellie said. "Afterwards."

"And Brom?"

"Brom left. He couldn't stay here then."

"Do you know where he is?"

"No," Nellie said. And the way she was looking at him, he could tell it was true, and that he was trusted.

"And you two have been here ever since."

"It's our place," Caney said. "And we're here. Maybe Brom will come back one day."

After a short silence, Slocum said, "But there's more. Who is this man Miles you thought I was riding for, Caney?"

"Lander Miles was . . . is . . . he wants our place," the girl said simply.

Another moment settled onto them, and at last Slocum said, "So the cattle war isn't over yet."

Neither of them said anything to that. Obviously they were spent. He told them to go to bed then, that he would talk with them in the morning.

He was up early the next day, and there was coffee and breakfast waiting for him in the log house.

There wasn't much talk. He asked a few questions about Miles and his Rocking Box outfit, and why he wanted the Rourke place.

A strange part of him didn't want to leave, but he didn't let that stop him. They watched him saddle up. Then before he mounted his pony, he walked over and checked his shoeing job on the bay.

"Not bad," he said, and winked at Caney. "For a man with a sore arm."

She blushed, but didn't look away.

He took a long look at Nellie when he was up in his saddle, then with a nod he walked his horse out of the corral and on down the trail.

He had already indicated to them that he would be back. There was no need to put it in words now. There was no need to say it again.

He had originally been heading for the Lazy Water, feeling the need for some kind of change. The shooting at the Willow Creek stage depot before he ran into the Rourke girls somehow decided him on riding to Medicine Butte. The shooting had been one of those freak things where some snotty kid on the prod for a rep had called out the man seated at the same table, a man named Otis. Slocum had been puzzled when the kid started jawing with Otis, who, for that matter, was no longer a young man. The kid had ridden in with two of his buddies while the stage was changing teams and the few passengers were having a meal. Slocum had just happened by. His pony had thrown a shoe, and he was in need of some tools plus a new shoe.

After he'd shoed his horse he'd come into the depot, where the kid was going at Otis. Otis had turned to Slocum. "Can this kid be turned off, Mister? I got no argument with him, nor with his buddies."

But the kid wasn't going to waste time in palaver. He went for his gun; and it was at that instant that Slocum caught on. In that sudden-death second he drew his own Colt and drilled the kid, then caught the slug in his arm from a bullet fired by Otis that had ricocheted off the cast-iron stove.

"Shit," said Otis, when he saw what had happened.

The kid who had longed for a rep was dead, and the other two had thrown down their guns and thrown up their hands.

"I've a mind to kill these two sonsofbitches," Otis said, blinking his eyes fast. "I got no idea why they was gunning for me."

The two kept their hands high. "We're out of it, mister," the taller one said to Slocum. "It was Hendry's notion. We just went along."

"How did you know I was here?"

"Spotted you riding in. The kid did; he was in the outhouse. Come rushing out 'fore he'd even buttoned his pants, he was that excited. I mean it! Thought you was Scarf Sables."

"What the hell's going on here?" Otis had demanded. "The sonofabitch braced me, not you!"

"That was to put me off guard. He almost did, but not quite. Some people want a rep pretty bad." Slocum's arm hurt. He looked hard at the two young men. They couldn't have been more than nineteen.

The shorter one was actually shaking. "Get out of here," Slocum said, "but leave your guns."

When the sound of their horses' hooves was dying away, he turned to the man named Otis.

"Reckon I'm gettin' on a bit," Otis said.

"So are we all," Slocum said drily. "You heading for Medicine Butte, Otis?"

"Yeah," he said, then suddenly wiped his nose with the back of his wrist. "You?"

"Just heading for the Lazy Water for a spell. But I might take in Medicine Butte."

Otis nodded, "You'd better see to that arm first."

"It's just a scratch," Slocum said, but with Otis's help he washed out the flesh wound and bound it with his bandanna.

Five minutes later he was riding down the trail, and it was only a few hours later that he was shot off his horse by Caney Rourke. It had turned out to be a busy day: two gun encounters, plus being mistaken for a man like Scarf Sables.

Now, in the Buffalo Bar in Medicine Butte, only a short time after the shooting contest, two men, slightly crouched, faced each other in front of the long mahogany bar. The barkeep, a man named Highpockets Purdy, stood frozen with his hand on the bar rag, halted in the very act of wiping. Philosophical, like so many of his trade, Highpockets simply awaited the inevitable.

Felix Horne, the marshal of Medicine Butte, was rigid with anger as he stood facing Burke Tobin. "I'll have a drink with you, Burke. But by God you take back what you just called me and hand over that gun!"

Burke, a sometime gambler and a sometime night rider, let out a guffaw of laughter and waved his Navy Colt at the lawman. Whereupon Horne cracked the recalcitrant and drunken Tobin right in the jaw, knocking him back into the bar, where he slid along the edge, knocking over bottles and glasses and crashing into some of the clientele, who hastily got out of the way. Then he stumbled against a spittoon and fell, still holding his handgun. From the floor he fired three shots, killing the marshal instantly.

Immediately—and, Slocum noted, at a signal from Shiner Ratigan, who was across the room—two bartenders jumped on the killer and carted him off to a back room.

"Harry, go get Sindall," snapped Ratigan. "Benjie, you tell them to tie him up good." The owner of the Buffalo Bar nodded in the direction of the back room. "And some men—you two there—carry the marshal to the icehouse and tell Lem Fang to get to work on a pine box." He turned, facing the gaping clientele, his hands raised in the sign of peace, his voice soft, persuasive. "It's all taken care of, everybody. Get on back to your drinking and gaming, and, uh"—with a sly smile as he let his eyes fall on a youthful hostess—"other things."

Slocum had to admire it. It all worked fine as a new pistol. Laughter bubbled up, the drinkers jostled each other as they turned again to the bar, the gaming clientele returned their attention to cards, dice, and faro. And those who were in pursuit of more fleshly attractions went back to where they had left off during the interruption.

Slocum had edged up to the bar and ordered a beer. He had already spotted the winner of the afternoon's shooting match, surrounded by bibulous admirers, including some women, at the far end of the long mahogany bar.

When he saw Shiner Ratigan approaching him, he turned to face him. "Reckon that wasn't part of the show, Ratigan."

"Sure wasn't."

"Adds a special something to the Fourth," Slocum said drily.

"I sure was wrong on that shootin' feller," Ratigan said. "Feller's a ringer, I guess. Working with that one taking those bets."

Slocum's face was as innocent as a baby's as he looked directly at Ratigan. "I would never have thought a man like you could be fooled like that," he said, and his voice was easy as a preacher's.

Ratigan had to grin at that. "I always heard you was a shrewd one, Slocum. Say, I'm looking for a good man—a smart one, handy with a gun, and with backbone."

Slocum leaned against the bar, letting his eyes rove over the crowded room. The noise filled the place. There was almost no air; the tobacco smoke all but obscured the ceiling. From another room came the tinkling of a honky-tonk piano.

"Looks to me like you got everything you need right now," Slocum said.

"How about a whiskey?" Ratigan said suddenly. "Make it a boilermaker."

"Depends."

"Not trail stuff. . . . Highpockets," he called to the bartender, "break out a drink for me and Mr. Slocum. Add me a beer."

Highpockets already had his hand on the bottle beneath the counter.

"That'll put lead in your gun," the saloonkeeper said as the bartender sloshed a generous portion into the two tumblers he'd placed in front of his special customers. Then he added a glass of beer for his boss.

"I've got almost everything I want right now," Ratigan said, picking up on the conversation that had been interrupted. He moved closer to Slocum. "I got an office in the back where we can talk." Lifting his tumbler of whiskey, he waited for Slocum to do likewise; and they drank.

Then Slocum followed him to the other side of the big room and through a door.

"It'll be quiet in here, and private," Ratigan said, putting his beer and whiskey on the one table, and nodding to Slocum to take a seat.

"I'm not really in the way of looking for work right now," Slocum said. "Especially your line." And he threw his thumb over his shoulder toward the room they had just left.

"No, nothing like that, my friend." Ratigan ran his hand over his face and then held it there, looking at Slocum over the edge of his palm. Then, moving his hand away, he said, "I need someone who can handle cattle, horses, and men. And a gun."

"I don't hire my gun."

"Of course not. Of course not!" He held up his palm in a placating gesture. "No offense, Slocum. I meant the kind of man who can handle horses, cows, men, but ain't afraid to back his play with a gun in a fair way. You get me now?"

"I got you the first time."

"I know about you. You're the kind I need. The pay will be good. And you'll have a fairly free hand. Course, you'd have to answer to me, since I'd be paying you."

"I didn't know you were in the cattle business, Ratigan."

"Well, I ain't really. That's why I need you."

Slocum felt a funny feeling going through him. He hadn't really wanted to have a drink with Ratigan, but for some reason his curiosity had been piqued. And now, while he wanted to get up and end the conversation, something in him wanted to hear the other man out.

"Cattle, huh," he said thoughtfully. "Just whereabouts might this be taking place?"

"Can't say right now. The location don't matter too much. But maybe, well, maybe around the South Fork, if you know this country at all."

Slocum did know the country, and he did know that the country around the South Fork of the Lazy Water was a mess of box canyons, and no place for running cattle—unless for changing brands in those natural rock corrals. But he knew that Shiner Ratigan was not telling it straight, and suddenly he thought of Nellie and Caney Rourke and their outfit up on the North Fork. Could Ratigan simply have switched

"North" for "South" to throw him off? It was a wild thought for sure.

"What would you want me to do?" he said. "I'm not saying yes. I'm just asking."

"Sure. Sure, Slocum." The grin was oily, the response too quick. "I can give you the details in a day or two. I'm waiting on a couple of things to happen. It won't be longer than maybe a week, ten days. That's sure. I just wanted to feel you out, see if we could get together."

Slocum didn't say anything to that. He just sat there, looking at the other man.

"To start with, it'd be moving a big herd up to the mountains for summer feed."

"What mountains?"

"That's what I'm waiting on. Got to get passage through a couple of outfits. But it's no worry on it. Only I just got to get the word. Now, what do you say? I'd appreciate to know so's I could plan."

Slocum stood up, pushed his hat onto the back of his head, ran his hand over his forehead, then lifted his hat and settled it afresh on his head, lower over the forehead now. He nodded at the still-seated Ratigan. "I'll turn it over."

"Good enough," Ratigan said, looking up at the tall man. "Give it a day or two?" he said, questioning.

Slocum didn't say anything. He didn't even nod. He turned and walked to the door, opened it, and went out. He had hardly touched his drink.

As he walked through the barroom to the swinging doors leading out to the street, two men were carrying the dead marshal through the parted crowd. And two others, with drawn guns, were escorting the man who had shot him under the watchful eye of a man with a star on his shirt, whom Slocum took to be the marshal's deputy.

3

After leaving the Buffalo Bar, Slocum walked down
to the livery to check his horse. He forked him some
hay and poured part of a can of oats into the bin for
him.

There was no one in the livery, not even the hostler, whom Slocum had hoped to have a word with.
But he couldn't find the man anywhere. So he
walked back uptown and watched the crowd that had
gathered for the prizefight out back of the Shirley
Hotel. Here there was even livelier betting than there
had been at the morning's shooting match. And here
he also spotted Shiner Ratigan, accompanied by two
other men. And Slocum realized again that Ratigan
always had men around him—some close, but some
others hanging about at a distance. The man was
smart, and Slocum knew that he had to be up to
something big, something a lot more than the run-of-

the-mill prizefight or shooting match. Something maybe with cattle.

And then to his astonishment who should he see as the referee of the Great Fight for the Championship of America but the unexpected winner of the morning's shooting contest. His name, it turned out, was Tice Finnegan. The man was clearly right at home, and while he was still a new face in town, the crowd accepted him with a great roar. Slocum strongly suspected the hand of Shiner Ratigan at work. Undoubtedly the fight was already fixed; as, just as undoubtedly, Mr. Tice Finnegan was on the Ratigan payroll.

Tice was nattily dressed this time—no more of the hayseed look, the bib overalls and hickory shirt and clodhopper shoes he'd sported at the shooting contest. Instead he wore a waistcoat over his striped shirt, even though it was a sweltering day, garters on his sleeves, and a six-shooter at his hip. He looked like a pygmy next to the two bruisers, yet not only Slocum but the crowd saw swiftly that Tice Finnegan was running the show.

His voice was much bigger than his body, and it carried to the edges of the crowd and beyond, where a number of men were standing on nearby roofs and the tops of porches.

Slocum spotted Ratigan then, at ringside, and he wondered which hunk of muscle he'd bet on. Without question, whoever was picked as the designated winner would assuredly be Shiner Ratigan's man. Slocum was beginning to wonder what other areas of Medicine Butte Ratigan had sewed up. He would have bet not a few.

He had a good view and he could hear Tice Finnegan clearly as he introduced the fighters to the excited throng and gave them their instructions.

"It'll be a fair fight. No biting, gouging, kicking, or walking on the other man's feet. No hitting below the belt. No knees, no elbows. And you do what I say. This here"—and he patted the gun at his hip—"will be the decider if you got any notion to argue with me. Now get to your corners and come out fightin'!"

As the fighters went to their corners, the crowd pressed in. Tice warned them back, his voice cracking over their heads like a whip over the backs of a cattle herd.

The fighters, whose names were Yankee Bill Sullivan and Boston Joe Sullivan, were obviously not related, though they had the same surname. Boston Joe was a head taller than Yankee Bill, who on the other hand was more than a head wider—or so it seemed to Slocum, who was enjoying himself.

Someone hit some kind of a pan at a signal from Tice Finnegan, and the fight started. Yankee Bill rushed out of his corner, obviously intending to sweep his opponent into oblivion, only to be met with a long, overhand right, brought up from Boston Joe Sullivan's shoelaces, which landed on his jaw. Yankee Bill fell like a tree, flat on his back with his arms outstretched, to all appearances out of this world.

A stunned silence enveloped the crowd while Boston Joe stood waiting with his fists in punching position, just in case his opponent should rise, while over the prostrate gladiator Tice Finnegan's sleeved arm rose and fell with the sweep of Father Time's scythe.

At the count of ten his right hand was already on the butt of his six-gun, while with his left he raised Boston Joe's arm, proclaiming him the winner by a knockout.

A tremendous roar broke instantly from the unbelieving crowd, which was now actually a mob as it swarmed toward the ring, intent on mayhem. Tice fired his six-gun in the air and bellowed caution into the faces of the leaders, but to no avail. Even he was forced into retreat as the great herd of enraged humanity screamed out cries of "Fake," "Fixed," and "Kill the sonsofbitches!" Bullets now laced the air. The ring ropes were cut and the platform was mounted as the mob clawed its way toward the two gladiators.

But those pugilists were not as dumb as they looked. Yankee Bill, who had been prone upon the floor of the ring, was on his feet almost at the first roar of the furious crowd and was now racing after the rapidly departing Boston Joe, who was heading down Main Street. Boston Joe raced into the Stand & Deliver Drink and Gambling Parlor, where he had left his clothes, while Yankee Bill tore like a dynamited buffalo straight to the livery stable. For a man of his great girth he was incredibly fast. In moments —and before the crowd reached him— he was out of the livery, riding a neat little buckskin who was surprisingly fast. Nobody gave even a thought to following him. After all, it was the Glorious Fourth, and there wasn't going to be anything to drink out there on the trail after everybody got himself a horse and tried to catch Yankee Bill.

Although there was indeed one dissenting view at this point.

"That's my buckskin the sonofabitch is riding!" said a tall, skinny man with a nose like a cant hook and a pair of black beady eyes, plus two big Navy Colts in tied-down holsters just inches from his two hands. He was wearing a tight-fitting black vest, and when he turned now, Slocum's eye was quick enough to catch the glint of metal just at an edge of that piece of clothing. He was, in fact, dressed totally in black, and John Slocum was pretty damn sure he was looking at Scarf Sables, the gunfighter the three kids at Willow Creek had mistaken him for. It did give him an interesting moment.

As Slocum settled down in the big iron tub of hot water in the back room of the town's barber parlor, he luxuriated at how relaxed he felt. A good hot tub sure beat diving into a creek or a mountain lake and jumping out and breaking the icicles off your body. Slocum was enjoying himself. It crossed his mind that he might enjoy a cigar when the voice suddenly cut in on his reverie.

"Sir, would you like a cigar? Or would you like to have your back scrubbed?"

The voice came from behind him. It took a good amount of control for him not to turn around, for his astonishment was like a piledriver in him. The voice had been absolutely clear, spoken in a soft though compelling tone. Slocum absolutely refused to turn his head as the girl walked into his line of vision. "You the barber?" he asked.

"Sometimes a customer might have trouble washing his back," the girl said. "So I'm here to help out. Adolf does the barbering and shaving."

Slocum lay back in the tub, feeling the familiar stirring in his loins as they exchanged looks.

She was about twenty-five, with green eyes, full red lips, carrot-red hair, a great mass of it piled on top of her head, and delightful ears, with small lobes from which small earrings hung. Her neck was long and smooth, her bare arms were obviously soft, and the way she moved them as she reached to the bench for a cake of soap excited him particularly. A turquoise silk dress more or less covered the rest of her body, though as she bent forward to reach the soap one marvelous bare breast came within inches of his face.

Without a word, Slocum simply leaned forward so that she could scrub his back. Her strokes were long, gentle, and lingering. His erection was all but plunging out of the water. As she worked she hummed softly, and he caught the scent she was using. Not strong, but a definite smell that seemed to be just right for her.

She worked slowly.

"Lift your arms," she said, as though talking to a child who was being led through routine.

He did so, and she washed carefully.

"Sit up more. There. That's it."

She washed his chest.

"Now lie back and lift your legs, one at a time." And she gave a little laugh.

He did exactly as he was told, wondering how she was going to handle the important parts of his body.

All the while, she kept her distance, her smile friendly yet not intimate.

"I think that's about it," she said. She had been kneeling beside the tub, and now got to her feet and reached for a towel and began drying her hands.

"What about the rest?" he said.

"That's your job."

"Boy, that's some service you give, miss," Slocum said, grinning at her. "I'll bet you get a lot of business."

"I do make a living." She had turned away from him and was looking at herself in the big mirror on the side table.

"You don't need that mirror," Slocum said.

"Really! I take that as a compliment, sir." And she turned to face him, laughing.

"That's how it was intended," he said. "Now, why don't you come on in here and join me."

She reached up to her shoulder and untied the strap that was holding up her dress. "I was only waiting for you to ask me," she said.

In the same moment, her dress fell to the floor and she was standing before him absolutely naked. As his erection charged fiercely out of the water her eyes swung toward it. "So that's where you've been hiding!"

And as she climbed into the tub with him, she was laughing. Sinking down on top of him, one breast found his hand, the other his mouth, while she spread her legs so that her crotch ran down the length of his erection. Then she lifted her buttocks and sank down onto him again, but this time with his bone-hard organ sliding all the way up into her. At the same moment their mouths came together, their tongues licking each other, driving into each other's mouth, searching, then sucking, while their pumping loins moved faster. Until at last neither could stand another second without release, and so they came. They came mightily, splashing water all over the room, charging into the sides of the heavy metal tub, until finally their passion spent itself totally.

They lay entwined, their faces just above the water so that they could breathe and not drown.

For some moments they lay still, dozing. She was still on top of him, though she had moved as his cock had softened and withdrawn.

After some more moments Slocum stirred, and, looking down her back, his eyes felt over the divided mounds of her bare wet buttocks.

"Oh, how delicious," she murmured, speaking into his neck. "I knew you had a big one, and I knew you knew how to use it."

"I knew it too," Slocum said.

"My name's Ginny," she said.

"My name's—"

"Slocum," she cut in before he could say it.

Slocum's organ began to stir beneath the water.

"There's something floating around down below the water," she said.

"It ain't floating, ma'am."

"I want you on top of me this time."

Slocum had already shifted his position and was now lying on top. His arm was sore from hitting the side of the tub, but he didn't care.

"I'm afraid we're getting Adolf's bathroom all wet."

"Fuck it," Slocum said gently into her ear.

"No," the girl said. "Fuck me."

Which he proceeded to do.

Slocum was a man who had the good sense to know it wasn't necessarily the man at the top, the success-ful rancher, miner, real estate land speculator to whom he might go for the best—that is, the most useful—information regarding a particular field. Gossip, he knew, as just about everyone else knew, was cheap and not wholly reliable by a long shot, but unlike others, he also knew that in gossip there often lay a kernel of truth, unalloyed by the need for prov-ing a point that was customarily the routine of the successful entrepreneurs of the West. It was among the barbers, carpenters, livery stable hostlers, whores, saloon swampers, and bartenders that he more often found gems than among the pile of fakes, who seldom delivered the genuine article.

Thus, he found himself in time chatting with one Lemuel Fang, a retired cabinetmaker who now kept his hand in by building pine-box coffins.

It was an especially appropriate moment for the conversation because of the hasty demise of Marshal Felix Horne, who, being a servant of the law, de-served, as Lemuel Fang put it "only the best."

"The marshal was an important man in town, I reckon," Slocum said. "I mean, I see everybody pretty upset by his getting shot up."

"That is true!" The cabinetmaker and coffin

builder brought the words out with the finality of Scripture.

Slocum's eyes rested on the large sign that was nailed—unevenly, he noted—above the door to the carpenter shop: "Within these portals man finds his last abode—Lemuel Fang, Builder of Coffins."

Slocum thought it was a nice touch.

"You favor that sign there, do you?" The old man looked up from his work on the marshal's coffin, cocking a watery blue and yellow eye at his visitor.

"It's nice sentiment," Slocum said carefully.

"Don't know that word, but it sounds good," said Fang, and bent to his work.

After a moment of silence, he spoke without looking up. "You bringing me business, or just want some jawin'?"

"Wondered if you knew a man name of Otis Dooley."

"Nope."

Slocum said nothing to that, only took a quirly out of his shirt pocket and lit up. It tasted good in the fresh morning air.

It was early, and while the town was definitely awake and about, there was still that early-morning ease and openness in the air that Slocum always favored, a time when people weren't as guarded as they inevitably were later in the day—that moment before things got into their habitual rhythm. People were still feeling out their bodies, checking the sounds that came to them, even wondering perhaps about the morning—the weather, the chores. Or—better—just wondering.

It was good standing there as the morning warmed

itself, watching the old man building the coffin. Nearby a door slammed and a dog started barking.

"You do other cabinet work," Slocum asked, "or just those permanent residences?"

"Why? You got something?" The old man canted his head fast at his visitor, one eye closed, the other open wide as a five-year-old's.

"Nothing. Just asking. I admire good, clean work in a man, and that's why I been watching you. On the other hand, if you don't want company, say so."

Lemuel Fang chuckled at that, then broke into a gruff laugh, followed by coughing, then spitting and hawking, then more laughing, finally dying off in a cackle.

"Tetchy, stranger, ain'tcha? I seen you at the shooting match, standing there next to Shiner Ratigan, looking like a hot licorice wouldn't melt in your mouth."

"How else can a man look when he's sitting in the middle of a stripping that obvious?" Slocum asked with a big grin of appreciation at the old man's observation.

"Reckon." He put down the hammer he'd been using and picked up a hand plane. "Reckon." He sniffed, pursed his lips, and squared off in front of his work. "I picked you first as a lawman, maybe a regulator," he said, speaking as he continued to work, without looking at Slocum. "Figured you were snoopin' around at somethin'. You didn't look dumb enough or dirty enough to be one of them waddies off of one of the outfits hereabouts, and I didn't know of any new herd coming in. Figured maybe you was a regulator for Miles and his bunch."

"Miles, huh?" Slocum gauged the tempo and tone of his exclamation so that it would simply grease the conversation along the way he wished it to go. And he remembered Caney Rourke taking him for one of Miles's riders.

"Lander Miles," Mr. Fang said. He stood back then, still holding the plane in both hands, and squinted at his visitor, who was now sitting on an upended crate.

"Then it come to me who you were, and about then too I heard the name Slocum. Don't ask me whereat. So I figured you was either just passing through or maybe only minding your own business, which I could be doing." And he turned back to his work and began planing the edge of the board that he had recently nailed in place.

"What can you tell me about Lander Miles?" Slocum asked. "Some friends of mine mentioned his name."

"Nothing."

"Name of Rourke," Slocum said, watching the old man closely. "Nellie and Caney Rourke."

Lemuel Fang kept working. "Who you throwed in with, mister?"

"Myself. And Nellie and Caney Rourke."

Lemuel kept right on working, and Slocum realized his voice was lower now. He could just about hear him.

"I got two things to say to you, Mr. Slocum. One, go easy on that name, what you just mentioned. And two, don't ask me no more questions."

Slocum stood up. "Thanks," he said.

The old man stopped planing and looked up. "What for?"

"You told me just what I want to know."

Lemuel Fang nodded. A curt nod. "Always heard you was a smart one, Slocum. And I can see it is so."

And he turned back to his work.

Slocum tossed away his quirly and started down the street. He heard a baby crying. Somewhere an upstairs window slammed open. A drunk came reeling out of the Golden Dollar Saloon, cackling at some internal monologue perhaps. Falling against the nearest hitching post, he began waving his arms, claiming that someone had stolen his horse.

Well, it was clear to Slocum now, after his encounter with Lemuel Fang, that the situation was grave. The carpenter had certainly told him what he wanted to know. How bad it was, which was plenty. And furthermore, he was beginning to catch on that that cunning bunco artist Shiner Ratigan was somehow running the whole show, or at any rate a big chunk of it.

Ulysses Ratigan had been born in Alabama and grew up to manhood during the turmoil of the War Between The States. He enjoyed the lively rumor, put out and fueled by himself, that he was the scion of a prominent Southern family, though such was not factually so. All the same, his Dixie background gave much toward a soft demeanor, a smooth, honeyed accent, and a courtly manner that were of uncountable value in convincing the innocent and the unwary that he was indeed a man who came from good stock, a man of probity and cultivation.

He had drifted west, like so many young men following the war. In Texas he had worked as a cowboy, joining a drive north on the Chisholm Trail. And it was then that he decided that never again would he engage in lowly toil. And for· the next twenty-five years he had practiced, sharpened his techniques, honed his routines for just such a situation as he had encountered when he arrived in Medicine Butte. Shiner Ratigan was determined that Medicine Butte would be his greatest game, a game in which he would put all that he had learned, suffered, and invented over the years.

In Abilene the youthful Ratigan had met a man named Hoskins, who taught him the coin-in-the-cake game. It was as old as the hills, as the saying goes. And like all con games, the coin-in-the-cake game ran on the principle that a very great number of human beings were simply loaded with avarice. The cake salesman—it could be pieces of pie—gathered a crowd around him and then began his spiel that the cake or pie that he was selling had been baked by a superb French chef, who because of his fame had found it necessary to keep his name secret for fear of being overwhelmed with orders for his product.

The Ratigan spiel on the quality of the product was superbly relaxed, yet gripping—even mesmerizing. The attention of the onlookers was completely caught. As he talked, he would wrap the pieces of pie or cake in colored paper, slipping banknotes of varying denominations into some of the cakes and then placing them in a big basket in such a way that

the marks thought they could easily spot where each
of the lucky cakes was.

Ratigan's hands were sheer poetry in their swift
and accurate and wholly mystifying movements, as
their owner massaged his audience almost to their
knees with wonder and greed. The con, of course,
was to pretend to put the money into certain pieces of
cake while in fact slipping it into others, whose
wrappers he then folded in such a way that they
could easily be spotted by his shills in the crowd.

When he was ready, Ratigan would offer the
unwrapped cuts of cake for twenty-five cents and the
wrapped cake at five dollars a slice. Immediately one
of his shills would step forward and lay five dollars
for a wrapped cake on the table top, barrel head, or
whatever flat surface Ratigan was using, then open
the brightly colored package and with a roar of dis-
covery and delight pull out a twenty-dollar bill and
wave it around for all to see. Following this dramatic
play the marks fell like locusts on the little packages.
None of these hopefuls ever got anything more than a
piece of pie or cake, though if one of these unfortu-
nates was silly enough to issue a loud complaint he
duly received something more than what he had bar-
gained for—in the form of knuckles, knees, elbows,
and other such "gentlemanly" weapons short of a gun
or knife.

With the money he earned in this adroit and color-
ful fashion Ratigan was able to start expanding his
operations and to collect a tight group of experienced
and highly polished con men and thugs around him.
In a word, professionals. He began visiting the new
silver camps, railroad tent towns, and cattle towns,

and soon he was running fake businesses, salting mines with fake gold and silver deposits and selling out for heavy money. He also ran fake lotteries and issued worthless stock by the thousands. These enterprises were the best and the simplest, and at these he excelled.

It was in Silvertown, a booming hamlet with no law or even a suggestion of government, that Ratigan honed some of the strategy and tactics that were to serve him so fully in his present situation at Medicine Butte. Since there was no law or government in Silvertown, he had simply enlarged his gang of "regulators," moved in, and taken over the town, declaring martial law. He forthwith set up a town government in which his own men held every office from mayor to chief of police and on down the line to coroner— this last office one in which a man of shrewd and careful action was essential.

But time, temper, and simple history had brought the end to this golden-egged goose. The mines ran out, and the town went down. Ulysses Ratigan was not a man to taste defeat for any great length of time. Somewhere along the way he had picked up the name "Shiner," and though the word in general use referred to a cardsharp using a certain device so that he could read another player's cards, Ulysses liked the name. It seemed to go with Ratigan much better than the name Ulysses. In appropriating it he managed somehow to give the word a status that it had never previously enjoyed. It mattered not at all that the word "shiner" was associated with dirty card play; it mattered that it was associated with the name Ratigan. By his use of the word he did not exactly change its meaning, but he certainly modified it and gave it a new impetus in the vocabulary.

And it was here in Medicine Butte that Shiner realized his great opportunity lay. He would do what he had done in Silvertown, only more. Here in Medicine Butte it wouldn't be just the government that he took over—it would be everything.

The early morning light was just passing through the dirty window glass and spreading through the office in back of the Buffalo Bar as Shiner Ratigan sat alone with his morning mug of coffee, his cigar, and a deck of cards with which he was practicing cuts and second deals. On the table in front of him was a brand-new holdout pistol he had received from the noted supplier of gambling advantage tools, as they were called, the E. N. Grandine Company.

He heard the step just outside the door, and the light though not hesitant knock.

"Come in," he said, and his hand swept the Grandine holdout out of sight into his lap.

"Come in, my dear." He looked up, smiling. "You look as bright as a morning jay, ready for a hot cup of coffee."

"I already told Highpockets to bring me one. That is, if you want company. Otherwise, I can . . ." She let her words disappear into her slow smile as she picked up on his mood.

"My dear, I can think of nothing I would like more than coffee with you. Did you sleep well?"

She was blond, with her hair falling onto her shoulders, which were bare. The rest of her was covered in black satin, which to Shiner's great pleasure showed off her youthful figure with amazing emphasis in just the right places.

Shiner, always the Southern gentleman, rose swiftly, remembering to grab the holdout in his lap, and offered her a chair.

"I see you're hard at work early in the morning," the girl said as there came another knock at the door.

"Come in," said Shiner again, not as softly this time.

Highpockets Purdy, the bartender, walked in carrying a mug of coffee and a pot of extra for his boss. Shiner had swiftly disposed of the holdout by shoving it under his coat, which was lying on another chair. Advantage tools were an accepted part of any gambler's equipment and were nothing to be ashamed of, but Shiner preferred that his employees —and for that matter his victims—had the notion that a man of his status could do it all without any such assistance.

"I have a visitor coming in this forenoon," Shiner said to the barman as he waited at the door. "Bring him in, but don't let anybody see you do it."

Highpockets, a spunky little man with a ready wit, gave a little salute with his forefinger to indicate he'd received the message all the way. Nor did he make the foolish mistake, as indeed he had early on, of asking the party's name.

When he was gone, Shiner poured more coffee into his mug. Then, sipping, he let his eyes play over his companion's face, her blond hair, her neck, and her bosom, which was straining against the black satin.

"I wish there was time, my dear."

"So do I," she replied, smiling at him. "When is your visitor due?"

"Pretty soon now. He'll be coming into town on horseback, so there's no knowing the exact time." He was studying her carefully, feeling his passion rising with each breath. "On the other hand, my sweet Vera . . ." He paused, as though the idea or suggestion he'd wanted to bring up was not appropriate to the present situation.

"I love the way you play with me," she said.

"I wasn't playing with you, my dear."

"Yes you were, Bunny."

Shiner Ratigan felt something odd passing through him as she mentioned her special name for him. He generally did, except for those times when he was so steeped in passion that a thunderbolt would have had no effect on him. "If we go upstairs, my dear, my visitor may come."

She rose suddenly and walked to the door and turned the key. Turning back to him, she held up the key and then popped it down between her breasts. "I can play too, Bunny." And her smile lighted up the whole of her face and gave a new atmosphere to her body as she came toward him.

He started to rise, saying, "Let's go upstairs."

"I want it here," she said.

"That's better. I don't care for everyone to be knowing my business, as I've often said."

He was all the way up from the chair now, and she put her hands on his shoulders so that he would sit back down.

"The floor's dirty, I'd ruin my dress."

"Where there's a will there's a way," Shiner said

as he settled back in his chair and spread his legs.

She had dropped to her knees and, reaching over expertly, she unbuttoned his trousers. It wasn't easy getting his erection out, but she didn't give up.

Then she was down on him. And for Shiner Ratigan nothing else mattered. Not his saloon, not the town, not his important visitor due any moment now. The only thing of any moment was the lovely girl sucking him and licking him and driving him right out of his mind. "My God," he murmured. "I'm going to come!"

She mumbled something in reply, but he couldn't make out what it was. Her words were inarticulate, for her mouth was full of his cock.

Yet he took it for agreement. And even if he hadn't, it would have made no difference, for he was already coming, cascading it down her throat, all but choking her as she continued to suck and lick and moan with happiness. He continued to come until he had released every drop, but she kept on sucking until his organ was as limp as a rag.

4

Once again the sun was hot on his back. He could feel his feet sweating inside his boots. And his saddle horn was hot to the touch. Under him the spotted pony sweated and gave off his thick horse smell. There was a hot wind, but in spite of it sweat ran down his face. Every now and again he lifted his hat and readjusted it on his damp head.

Slocum kept watching the horizon ahead, careful, taking his time, using the point of his hat brim as a marker, studying all the tight corners and edges of the rimrocks ahead, and also looking far out on either side. As best he could see there were no outriders. Well, maybe he wasn't all that close yet. But they'd show soon, of that he was certain. Lander Miles was definitely not the man to leave invitations for intruders.

The sky held nothing in it. Not a single bird, not a

wisp of cloud. It seemed there was even no air. Yet there were waves of heat. His horse stirred up an amber-colored dust as he pursued the lazy trail across the expanse of prairie that led to the higher country.

After a while he rode into the first canyon, his eyes smarting some from the dust. His pony's shod hooves rang now on the rocky trail, and echoes coughed back from the high walls. To his right ran a creek through red sandstone. His eyes caught sight of bluestem, tall but not stirring in the dead heat. The smell of sage was rich, almost burning his nostrils like a medicine.

The heat seemed hottest when they stopped for water, both to drink and to cool themselves in the rushing, dancing creek. Without any hesitation Slocum shucked off his clothes and slipped into the water. He stayed close to the bank, within easy reach of his clothing, his guns—the Colt, the Winchester. His pony stood in the water over his hocks, drinking, while the creek swirled around his legs, cooling him all over.

Slocum dried himself in the air, dressed, checked his horse's rigging, and mounted.

In the late afternoon he rode up and over a low lip of green and brown land, and, looking across the great valley, he made out the rimrock under which the Rourke spread lay.

The outfit itself wasn't visible, and he admired the choice Rourke had made. From practically every side the place was protected. No one could come up close without being spotted. Not that any protection of that sort would hold off the standard cattle baron once he got his mind set on your land. But at least a man holding out in a gun battle over there at the Double R would go down with a good fight.

Slocum dismounted and studied the terrain through his glasses. The Rourke spread lay roughly halfway between Miles's Rocking Box and the lush pasture above on Elbow Mountain.

Now the question hit him again: Had Shiner Ratigan really gotten into the cattle business? Slocum chewed on it for several moments. True, Ratigan had only barely mentioned "something" on the South Fork; and that was nowhere near the Double R or the Rocking Box. But a man such as Shiner Ratigan could easily be setting a false trail, putting it the way he had, figuring Slocum would see through it, that it wasn't the South Fork he was interested in but the North. Hadn't he mentioned the problem of getting cows up onto the mountain for summer feed? Studying the layout across the valley, Slocum could see how that question could be right there before his eyes. To the east of the Rocking Box he could see where there had been a landslide, and so going that way with the Miles herd was impossible. There was only one route that the Rocking Box cattle could take to get up onto Elbow Mountain, and that was through the Double R.

Slocum studied the terrain a moment longer, then walked over to where his spotted pony was cropping the rusty-colored bunch grass. A meadowlark called as he picked up the reins, and then after checking his saddle cinch, he put his foot into the stirrup, grabbed a handful of mane in his left hand along with his reins, and mounted easily.

He took one last look at the place where the Double R was so well hidden, then turned his horse's head, kicked him in the belly, and continued on his way toward Lander Miles's Rocking Box spread.

Medicine Butte was a town of some thousand persons. It had one main street with frame houses and stores with false fronts lining both sides behind wood boardwalks. The street was wide, and in the noontime it now lay under a thick sheet of dust that had only just settled after the stage had come in, raising a tremendous cloud.

There was a courthouse, two churches, a sort of fire department with volunteers, a town marshal recently raised from deputy following the death of Felix Horne, a post office, a saddle shop, a harness shop, a hardware and general store, and seven saloons.

On this day Nellie Rourke had driven the spring wagon into town with a team of bays that her father had favored during his short lifetime. She made the purchases she and Caney had decided on, and by noon she was through and ready to head back to Elbow Creek. The spring wagon was loaded to its limit. Every now and again during her visit to the town someone would stop and greet her and ask after Caney. No one mentioned her brother, Brom, but it was clear to anyone who would have cared to notice that the citizens of Medicine Butte, including the shopkeepers she dealt with, were fond of the Rourke girls and concerned for their future. More than one, especially the older ones, had clucked about two such fine young girls living alone way out on the North Fork like that, with no man around for the heavy chores and for protection if need be. Still, no one had exactly volunteered to take on the job, to offer himself to whipsaw the Double R spread. "Best thing would be for that Nell to catch herself a husband who'd care for both girls and the ranch" was how it was often put.

For that matter, there were any number of possible suitors for someone as good-looking as Nellie Rourke. The only problem was that Nellie hadn't seemed to find any that suited her. Still, the gossip ran on, and the tongues amused themselves, while over the long period of time since the killing of Tom Rourke, Nellie and Caney continued to work their ranch as well as they could. Now and then a neighbor sent over a man to help out for a few days, but then gradually the excitement of the killing of Tom Rourke, and the killing of his killers, settled itself into the history of the town and surrounding country, and it was less often that anyone rode over to help out.

Every so often—maybe once a month—Nellie drove into town either in the spring wagon or leading a packhorse, leaving Caney at the ranch to handle things. This day wasn't any exception. As soon as she'd finished her purchases, with her wagon loaded, she drove up to the town trough and watered the team of bays, then tied them to the hitching rail in front of the post office.

Nellie always stopped by the post office before leaving town to go back to the ranch, and Caney always reminded her to do so as she waved her goodbye—to go to the post office in Sayles's Hardware & Clothing Emporium and see if there was any word from Brom. There never was, and this day was no exception. Nellie bore the expected news of no news with her customary dignity, as usual refusing to show her deeper disappointment in front of Mrs. Gravitsky, the postmistress.

When she came out into the street again she saw a man standing by her team and spring wagon. And seeing it was a stranger, she realized that she had been hoping to run into John Slocum.

"The name is Ratigan, Miss Rourke. Ulysses Ratigan," the man said, touching the brim of his hat and smiling pleasantly at her.

"Yes?"

"I was wondering if we could have a talk together, uh, privately."

She felt something tighten in her and tried now to show what she was thinking. Aware that she was flushing a little, she said calmly, "I'm sorry, sir, but I'm on my way out of town, and I can't stop now."

She made as though to move toward the hitching rail to untie the team, but he moved right along with her.

"Miss . . ." And this time he removed his hat completely, holding it against his chest in supplication. "Miss, I am in no way attempting to, uh, molest? if I may put it in that crude way. I am trying to offer you a business proposition."

It had not entered Nellie Rourke's mind that such a man would even think of "molesting" her, and being an intelligent girl she had to assume that indeed the thought had surely entered his.

"I am sorry, sir."

She stepped into the stirrup of the wagon and

swung up into her seat, holding the reins.

Shiner Ratigan, however, was not a man to be easily avoided. His hand reached out and held the near rein of one of the team. "I want to speak to you, but privately, about your Double R ranch." And seeing her rising reaction he swiftly added, "I happen to know that Lander Miles is interested, and may be applying a certain pressure or insistence to his suggestion or offer." He smiled and he opened his hands to invite, avuncular to the pores of his fingers and toes.

Nellie felt a chill at the mention of Lander Miles, but she was not taken in by the kindly-uncle attitude. Yet she restrained her impulse to pull the rein away from him, reasoning that she had nothing to lose by listening.

"I can give you a few moments, sir. To state your business. I want to get home before evening."

"But of course. Of course!" Shiner stood back, releasing the rein in an apologetic gesture. "I simply have to speak to you, and I do believe you'll see it's for your own good. And your sister's." He beamed, unction oozing from his coarse face, while his beady agate-colored eyes glowed at how he had won the round. "We can't talk here. But there is the On Time Cafe across the street. We could have some coffee."

He reached up to take the reins to wrap them around the hitching post, and with his other hand offered to help her down.

But she refused both gestures. Jumping nimbly to the ground, she kept hold of the reins herself and then wrapped them loosely around the post, as her father had shown her long ago.

In the On Time, Nellie looked at his agate eyes, the wrinkled face in which so many things could be hidden. Yet there was something kindly in those eyes. Why didn't she trust that? she asked herself. And she knew it was because the man had something else besides a surface kindness. His eyes seemed to feed on her, for one thing, and he was too quick with his words, as though always justifying his behavior.

"I have been aware of you and your sister out there all alone on your ranch," he was saying now, his words dripping with honey. "Mighty lonely for two young ladies, I'd been thinking."

"Mr. Ratigan, why don't you get to the point of what you want?"

Her directness hit him again, but he didn't let it show. All the same, a young girl like that, so young, so innocent, so—yes, by God—so desirable. She just had to be a Yankee. No civilized young woman in the South would ever be that direct. He had better be careful. His eyes moved slowly across her lips.

Then he said, "I have heard, as I said, that Lander Miles is trying to acquire your ranch. And since I have my hand in many of this town's functions, being on the Town Council and in other organizations, and so on and so forth, I hear things. I see things. And I simply wish to offer my services should you need help of any kind." This time he achieved the totally disarming personality that he had tried for—but damnit, she was so damned good-looking!—and had until now missed the mark. He saw her open to him a little. Her lovely blue eyes were somber.

"It's a big responsibility you and your sister

have," he went on, stroking the words. "It's hard, with no man to help you." He hesitated, about to mention the fact that with her brother gone it must be even more difficult, but wisely he refrained, fearing that mentioning Brom Rourke might spoil what he was working toward. He could see she was listening to him now, that, for the present anyway, her suspicions had been somewhat put to rest.

"I can't deny that it's been difficult, Mr. Ratigan," the girl was saying now. "But we have managed this far, and I expect we shall continue." And then she added, "It's kind of you to be concerned. I appreciate it, and I know my sister will too when I tell her."

"I have a good lawyer in my employ," Shiner said. "And should you ever need legal advice, he can be placed at your disposal."

"Thank you." She had hardly touched her cup of coffee, but now she stood up. "I really must be going."

And before he could say anything she was gone.

Shiner Ratigan continued to sit where he was, nursing his coffee and enjoying a fresh cigar. His thoughts were full of her youthful beauty, her freshness, and that charming directness that was almost yet not quite that of a mature woman. Indeed, it was much more sincere. And while he knew that this could be dangerous to his plan, at the same time he couldn't help but be attracted.

Shiner Ratigan felt a marvelous something stealing into his loins, and as he sat there with the sunlight throwing long rays across the town a smile came into his eyes, into his mouth, into his whole face. He would have to be careful, he told himself.

He knew very well his weakness. And he had to keep his eye on the action, and not be derailed by a pretty face, and those obviously glorious breasts. In the past he had made one or two "mistakes" while involved in one of his "games." But this time he was going to be careful. Women—pretty women—were wholly desirable. No question about that. And he had worshiped Beauty and Desire. And he would surely continue to do so. He smiled right into the sunlight that was now washing over the windowpane. Women! God's great gift to man. But so was money! So too was power!

Riding along easy now, of a piece with the spotted pony's motion, Slocum let his thoughts play over the events of the past few days. He wasn't sure how it had happened, but for some reason or other he now felt connected with those two girls out on Elbow Creek, felt their question, their problem in the face of what was shaping up as a struggle with the big Rocking Box outfit, even felt in a strange way that he had somehow shown up just for that purpose, at the exact time they needed him.

Why? He didn't know them, didn't know and hadn't known any of their kin. So why did he now feel beholden? It was a strange feeling, and he didn't spend a whole lot of time trying to explain it. He knew in his bones what it was, not so much in his head. He saw it as something that had come at a certain moment in his life and needed handling. He was like that—one of those who knew that there were sometimes certain things in a man's life that just had to be done. For no special reason.

They were loping along a narrow two-wheel trail close to a wide creek. Grass grew green on both sides of the streaming water. Now and again a high cut-bank held one or the other side of the swiftly flowing water as it ran through strips of sage and grease-wood.

Slocum could feel the sun going down behind him, felt it extra-warm on his back. Ahead he watched the high snowcapped peaks of the Wapiti Range.

Riding closer to the Rocking Box on Spring Creek, he watched the land flatten out ahead of him. Far to the west he saw a high butte standing alone in the graying light. Everywhere the shadows were lengthening. Except for the sound of his horse's hooves it was very still, very silent, a time when life and death were especially close.

He had no idea really why he had decided that it would be useful to ride out to the Rocking Box. To see the lay of the land maybe. Certainly not to meet up with Lander Miles or any of his hard riders. But to see what was involved close up. He had heard a good bit about Miles in Medicine Butte. And from what he could gather this was no man to spend your time with unless you were either all the way with him, or against.

But Slocum had a notion of riding over the land a bit, getting to know the way of it. He wanted to know exactly how a man like Miles would send a herd of cattle up onto Elbow Mountain, exactly what route he would take, and how long the drive would take. He also wanted to see what sort of feed the man was after. Slocum knew that in reading the way a man handled cattle, tools, and horses lay as sure a way as any of finding out who that man really was in his guts.

He was looking for outriders now, realizing he might already have been spotted. A man such as Miles wouldn't be taking any chances. He would have every corner of his big spread covered, every approach. And sure enough he suddenly caught the glint of something—a concha on some rider's saddle?—over to his right, and then in another moment spotted a rider against the skyline.

Slocum rode past a stand of cottonwoods on his left, followed by a bigger stand on his right. The late sun, as it struck through the cottonwoods, caught the gleam of water where two creeks met in the late-afternoon light.

In another moment he rode along a fringe of box elders lining a narrow creek, and crossing, he passed between two low buttes that suddenly opened out to a meadow where a herd of cattle were bunched.

Clearly they were being held for branding. Riders held the edges of the herd. Still in the protection of the box elders, Slocum watched the riders as they rode back and forth, cracking the ends of their lariat ropes like whips when any animal attempted to break out. Meanwhile, the roper, astride a big chestnut horse, was walking his mount into the bawling beeves, building himself a loop and then, easy as light, tossing it over the forequarters of the calf he'd selected, letting the animal walk through until he yanked up suddenly, with precise timing, tightening the rope over the calf's rear leg. His well-trained cow pony now began to pull back so that there was no slack in the rope, moving expertly to keep the lariat taut, while two men afoot hustled forward. One grabbed the terrified calf under one rear leg and around the neck and with a smooth heave dumped it on its side, knocking out its wind, kneeling hard on the desperate animal's neck, while his partner grabbed one rear leg and split it from its companion, as a third man swiftly castrated the bawling animal and then cut a notch in its ear. At the same time a fourth cowboy approached with a white-hot branding iron and burned the Miles brand into the suffering calf that was now a young steer.

Slocum always enjoyed watching roundup and branding. The ease of the hardworking men, the poetry of their flowing movements, where each knew exactly what to do, and he especially enjoyed watching a well-broken cow pony with a top roper working through the bawling, stomping herd. The din of the calves mothering up and the mothers searching for them, the choking dust, and the curses of the men seemed only to accentuate the serenity of the roper and his cow pony by contrast. Slocum remembered an old-timer telling him how roundup with a bunch of top hands reminded him of a dance in hell.

The sun was moving down rapidly now, and the branding was almost done. But the hands would remain there until the calves had all mothered up.

The light was still good. He had taken out his glasses and was watching the riders up close. They looked just like any branding team, and the cattle looked like any cattle you might find anywhere.

Except that suddenly through the glasses he caught something that looked like an "RR" brand.

Then he spotted the double R on two more beeves.

"Find what you're lookin' for, mister?" said the voice behind him. And that voice was as hard as the gun barrel that was pointing right at Slocum's back. "Turn slow, with your arms out to your sides."

There were three of them. Three hardcase, each holding a gun on him.

"You boys nervous?" Slocum asked easily.

"That we are," the one on the left said. "But Kane here, he asked you a question."

"I think he deserves an answer," said the third man, who had not yet spoken.

"Well, I did find what I was looking for, boys," Slocum said, his tone still pleasant. "Nice of you to ask."

"And that might be?" It was the first speaker again, Kane, the biggest of the three, a man with a red, beefy face, a thick beard, and tiny eyes that blinked a lot.

Slocum didn't answer. He had started to reach for the case to his field glasses when one of the men drew back the hammer on his six-gun.

"I'm putting the glasses back in the case," Slocum said, without the least hesitation in his movement.

"What you doin' out here?" one asked.

"I'm riding to the Double R, the Rourke outfit."

"You're a good piece off your way, mister," said another.

And the third one said, "We'll take that gun. Hand it over real easy like." And when Slocum drew the Colt carefully out of its holster, he added, "Hold it by the end of the barrel."

"But I'm aiming to stop in on Miles," Slocum said

suddenly, without handing the gun over. "You boys work for Miles?"

"What do you want with him?"

"My business."

It was a moment when the other two had dropped their guns back into their holsters, and only the speaker was covering Slocum.

"Kane, he don't look like anybody Miles wants to see," said the smallest of the three.

Kane, the big man with the big beard, let the hammer down on his cylinder, carefully, slowly.

"What do you think, Joey?" he said.

Joey, a man with a patch over his eye, spat over the side of his leg. "Think he seen anything?" he asked Kane. And then, when Kane shrugged. "What do you think, Dutch?"

Dutch, a squat man with short legs but a long trunk, sniffed. He had very hairy nostrils. "He's too damn smart for my money, boys. Let's string him up."

Slocum could see that they had been drinking— not very much, but there was a looseness in each of them that was obviously from drink.

"String him up. I honeys them glasses."

"You can have 'em," Slocum said easily, and he pulled them out of their case. "You want the case, too?"

"Not much good without the case," Dutch said. And he grinned, and with his right hand scratched under his armpit.

That was his mistake, the one Slocum had been angling for. As he lifted the glasses and slipped them back into the case, he watched the other two. Joey had turned to the man named Kane, who was still holding his gun on Slocum.

And then Slocum pulled the oldest trick in the book. "Jesus, what's that?" he said, staring wild-eyed past Dutch and Joey.

And just for that split second the two lost their attention. Dutch was still scratching his armpit as Slocum hurled the field glasses and case at Kane's hands. The hand holding the six-shooter moved, and the gun fired, the bullet hitting the sky. Slocum was still on his horse, but away from the trio, while his hand had sped to the hideout inside his shirt. He had it out and up and had the three covered. He had dropped the Colt back into its holster when they had spoken about stringing him up, and now he pulled it out and returned the hideout into his shirt. "Now we'll head for Mr. Lander Miles," he said.

They were suddenly flattened, realizing how their highjinks had turned them into utter fools. But Slocum knew that wouldn't last. He knew that shortly they would recover their anger, their justification. And it was just as he had this thought that he knew something else. "Who do you work for?" he asked suddenly on a hunch.

"Miles," Kane said, almost before Slocum had gotten the words out of his mouth.

"You're lying."

"Don't say that," the one named Joey said. But he couldn't hold to their former prisoner's hard look. "Used to."

"Got fired, I reckon, on account of the rotgut. Am I right, boys?"

They were silent, stewing in their own thoughts.

"Couldn't rightly say it was just like that," Kane said, his face looking suddenly beefier than ever.

"I am saying it," Slocum said hard, icing out Kane's attempt at easing his predicament. He made a motion with his handgun. "I'll be watching your backtrail, remember that."

Joey said, "We won't forget you, mister."

"Next time," Dutch said, and he glowered from beneath his chewed-out hat brim.

"Boys, just make sure there won't be a next time. I'm letting you off easy. Now git."

He sat the horse, watching them ride off three abreast down the trail. He knew what they were thinking, had been thinking while they had their guns on him.

Working for Lander Miles or not, it was pretty sure that the grim trio had it in mind that Miles would likely pay something pretty damn good if they could take him.

He sat there in the warm saddle watching them out of sight, realizing that this had been a turning point. Now *he* really had to watch his backtrail—night and day. For the word had clearly gotten around. And as he kicked his pony toward the Rourke spread he wondered what the connection was between Miles Lander and Shiner Ratigan.

5

Slocum's grim prediction was borne out almost too soon. He had ridden away from his encounter with Kane, Dutch, and Joey, ostensibly heading for the Rourke spread all the way across the valley. He had already seen enough outriders near the Miles outfit to convince him that Lander Miles was a man who thought of everything. And it was not beyond possibility that the cattleman had even sent Kane and his sidekicks to confront him, told them to play the role of having been fired, maybe to disarm him. Or, on the other hand, Miles might have had the three followed by yet other riders, who when Slocum's guard was down would hit him. As he rode down the long sweep to the Lazy Water River he thought of a number of possibilities. But by the time he crossed the river he was pretty sure he wasn't being followed. Several times he had stopped, dismounted, and erased any sign that would help a tracker, plus he had ridden over hard ground as much as possible and had ridden in the river and a couple of creeks to confuse any rider behind him. Every now and again he had stopped and studied his backtrail through the field glasses. Nothing.

He rode a long way around, even so. For one thing he wanted to get a close view of the land so that if he had to maneuver he wouldn't get in trouble. He found more than one interesting trail between the two outfits, plus of course the best route for driving cattle. Once again he spotted the Rourke brand on three or four head mixed in with Rocking Box cattle. Of course that could easily be a mistake, or they could have been placed there intentionally in order to provoke some kind of action from the two remaining Rourkes, although Slocum could not conceive of how the two Rourke women could possibly cause trouble with Miles and his big, tough Rocking Box gang. The two girls were helpless, and that had to be clear to everybody.

As he worked his way up through the tall timber on the other side of the river, taking full advantage of cover from any possible trackers, he thought of Lemuel Fang, Medicine Butte's carpenter-undertaker and, Slocum felt, a man who saw more, and probably knew more of what was really going on, than any man in town or its environs. But a man with a tight check rein on his mouth. He had definitely given him that impression when he'd met him the other day. He admired the way Fang had let him know the caliber of the situation in Medicine Butte and the surrounding country and outfits without saying one single word about it. A man like that was worth ten of any other kind.

It was with this thought in mind that after he had studied the physical layout of the Miles-Rourke standoff and what the best and worst possibilities were, he decided to head back to Medicine Butte.

He had found out what he wanted to, and though he regretted not stopping by to see Nellie and Caney Rourke, he listened more to his feeling that time was being measured. Miles wasn't going to wait forever; in fact, he knew the cattleman wasn't going to wait much longer, not with the branding already going on.

But by the time he came to the far opening through the thick timber, it was night. And to his agreeable surprise he came upon a small, tightly built log cabin. It was the kind of cabin frequently found in the mountains. No one lived in these small structures. They were actually stopovers along the trail for trappers, hunters, cattlemen—anybody riding the trail. Slocum knew these places and had often stopped in them. There was always the makings of dinner and breakfast and for building a fire.

This cabin was no exception. It had a dirt floor, and the walls and roof were solid, with tight chinking. There was flour, coffee, sugar, beans, and sourdough for trail biscuits. Travelers were expected to leave supplies when they departed, to see that there was firewood ready for the potbellied stove, to make repairs if necessary. Such places, Slocum knew, had saved the lives of more than a few men half-frozen and hungry on the trail, and maybe even lost.

He stripped his horse, rubbed him down briskly with some twigs, and fed him oats. There was a spring, and he watered him. Someone had completed a pretty makeshift corral: Slocum could tell a number of hands had worked on it at various times. He didn't hobble the spotted pony but left him in the corral, slipping the bit out of his mouth and moving the headstall back down on his neck, so that if necessary he could be bridled swiftly. Then he took the Winchester and his war bag and blankets into the cabin.

There was coal oil handy, and he lighted the lamp. There was kindling and logs, and he built a fire for cooking, deciding to stop for the night and ride in to Medicine Butte in the morning. He wanted to think things out. He kept thinking of those two Rourke girls all alone out there on the North Fork. They just had to be the target, even if there had been no Lander Miles. God, it was like some crazy storybook. True, there were often situations where women were left alone way out away from anyone else who could possibly help them with the tribes, the outlaws, or even just the saddlebums who might be passing through. And they had survived. Yet the two Rourke girls somehow seemed different to Slocum. He knew it wasn't just because he was hot for Nellie. The two of them just seemed so damned innocent. And the tough point was, he fully realized, that it was just because of their obvious innocence that they were such a target.

He rustled grub for his supper, then smoked a quirly, still thinking of the girls, Lander Miles, Ratigan, and old Lemuel Fang. He lay down on his bedding, fully clothed, with his weapons at hand. Just before dropping off to a light trail sleep he heard a coyote barking.

Something awakened Slocum. In the dark he could hear it scampering across the dirt floor. He raised himself in order to hear better, still on the alert for any Rocking Box men, or even the trio of Kane, Joey, and Dutch. Then he heard rustling. He reached to his hat and pulled a match from the hatband. He struck it on his thumbnail, one-handed, and it hissed into a small light. It was a pack rat, just disappearing through an opening between two bottom logs of the cabin. The lucifer went out, and Slocum lay back again, happy that it was still dark and he could get some more sleep.

It was just the first breaking of dawn when the heavy door of the cabin was shoved open and he came fully awake. Because it was still fairly dark inside the cabin he couldn't make out the face behind the gun that was pointing directly at him. He was aware too of a second man next to the one holding the gun.

For a moment Slocum feigned sleepiness.

"Get up," said the voice, hard as the gun barrel pointing between Slocum's eyes.

"Who the hell're you?" Slocum said, pretending to be yawning and still half asleep. He stretched, shaking his head, letting his hand come down closer to his handgun.

"It ain't gonna matter to you, Slocum. The boss wants to see you. Haul ass!"

"And right now!" said the voice of the second

man, who he could see now was also holding a gun on him.

Slocum pretended to have his eyes still closed as he yawned again, but he was actually watching the two figures standing by his bedroll. He thought they were maybe two of the trio he'd run off the day before, but he wasn't sure which two.

Almost with no effort, he made as if to move to get up from where he was lying on the ground, rolling to one side and in the same fluid motion sweeping the .45 into his fist and firing. One of the figures cursed, and the gun that was closest to Slocum fired, the bullet just missing his head and tearing into the heavy log behind him. The second gun fired then, the bullet driving into his bedroll where a moment ago he had been lying. The sharp smell of gunpowder and smoke filled the cabin. Slocum fired again, swinging to his knees and then to his feet, as both figures raced to the door of the cabin and made it outside.

Slocum was up and after them on the instant, firing as he pursued his quarry. But in the very nick of time, he remembered something from long experience, and as he came through the door he ducked and dodged to one side in the still-gray light as the bullets swept past him and were buried in the heavy logs. The trick had almost worked.

Suddenly a man jumped out from around the corner of the cabin and let fly with his handgun. His aim was not accurate, and Slocum spun and threw down on the man, knocking the gun out of his hand. Cursing, the man fled after his companions. And in just moments, Slocum made out the sound of galloping horses in the distance.

He ran quickly to the edge of the clearing and dropped into the thick timber and waited. They could be pulling the same trick again, riding out and leading him on, and into an ambush. But Slocum waited. He didn't fall for the possible ruse.

He waited a good while, then, after checking carefully where the man had mounted up, he returned to the cabin. He cooked up some breakfast, making a good amount of coffee, which he would take along with him and heat up later. It was easier that way. After seeing that he had left the cabin in good shape, he mounted up and rode toward Medicine Butte.

He had a lot of pieces to put together, and he had decided that he had to have a talk with Lemuel Fang. He needed background information, the kind only a man like Fang could give him.

Following that, there could be Lander Miles, and for sure Shiner Ratigan, but what Slocum lacked was the information that would indicate to him where and how and when Miles would move in closer to the Rourke girls. And Slocum knew there wasn't much time. He had no idea how he knew there was little time left, but he wasn't going to argue it, for as always he accepted his hunches. And so far he hadn't often come up wrong.

As luck would have it—or perhaps Slocum's "extra sense" was at work—he quickly discovered a way to loosen Lemuel Fang's tight tongue. It was the most obvious way in the book, naturally, he realized as they sat in the back of Fang's carpenter shop—

mortuary. It was Old Overholt, and it reached into all the places where a man might be hiding. Actually, Slocum realized that it was Fang's finally trusting him that melted the ice as much if not more than the booze. But the Old Overholt didn't do any hindrance, as he put it to himself.

It was a pleasant evening. The day's work, as far as the carpenter went, was done. There was still plenty of light coming through the small window that gave onto the alley. They sat on upended crates, passing the time, smoking a couple of good cigars that Slocum had brought along for the occasion, and trading anecdotes.

"They tell it that early on, down someplace in Texas—and what the hell ain't someplace in Texas? —that Shiner once bought up a helluva lot of beeves during an epidemic. He insured 'em, then infected 'em and collected the insurance." Lemuel Fang dropped both his eyelids solemnly over his protuberant blue-yellow eyes, innocent as a babe.

"I see Mr. Ratigan was a man who knew how to fend for himself from an early age," Slocum said drily.

"Still does, my lad. Shiner still does. And more so than ever. More power to him, I says, if that's the way of it."

"Nobody's complaining," Slocum said. "Just admiring the man's way of it."

Lemuel reached for the Old Overholt. He took a hefty swig, whistled out his breath, and belched whiskey, chewing tobacco, onion. Slocum gave thanks that he was in good enough condition to withstand the attack. This little action went blithely unnoticed by Lemuel Fang, who now beamed on his guest who had been kind and thoughtful enough to bring along such a savory bottle.

"Tell you about the one time in K.C. Shiner was pulled in by the Fire and Police Commission after two eastern real estate fellers claimed he'd snookered them out of two thousand dollars. Know how he got out of it?"

"I surely don't have a notion," Slocum said agreeably. "But I'll bet it was a good one."

"Shiner was runnin' his usual gambling house at the time, and that's where the greeners claimed they was taken. Well, Shiner, he got let off. You know how come?"

"Just told you I didn't. Tell me. How did he wiggle out of it?"

Fang chuckled into the neck of the Old Overholt bottle as he brought it to his wet lips. His eyes were laughing, and in fact Slocum noticed there was a ripple going through him. He just couldn't wait to come across with his story stopper. Like a little kid, Slocum thought.

The old man handed the bottle to his companion, leaned forward on his crate, with his hands on his bony knees, arms akimbo, as he wagged his big pink and white head. "Shiner got—what the hell they call it?—ak, ak-something."

"Acquitted?" Slocum put in politely. Yet he too was beginning to feel the power of the booze.

"Yeah, that's the one. Well, what I am saying is he got plumb off. Want to know how?" He cocked his head at his guest, like a bird, nodding slightly as he did so, "Old Shiner he's a corker. He argued it

with the firemen and police and the judge or whatever was there that, hell, he wasn't running a gaming
house at all but a education outfit, like that one they
call the Keely—you know, the one gets folks to quit
smoking or drinking or something." He was about to
continue, but his laughter overtook him and he
started to shake.

Finally he regained his breath enough to go on.
"See, Shiner was sayin' that some folks get a cure for
the drinking habit. Well, old Shiner, he told it that he
was giving people a cure for the gambling habit."

Both had a good long chuckle at that, and then
Lemuel Fang resumed. "Then by God he nailed 'er
down by pointing it out that in *his* place gamblers
didn't have a chance of winnin' on account of things
was fixed so's nobody could win. Fact, Shiner had a
big sign at the head of the stairs saying just that."

"What did the sign say?" Slocum asked.

"You speak Greek?"

"No. Leastways, not yet."

"Sign was written in Greek. But I am told it said
"Let the Buyer Beware." Lemuel paused to blow his
nose through his thumb and index finger—deftly,
missing Slocum's knee by at least two inches—and
then went on. "I was told that Shiner then said to the
judge—or whosomever it was runnin' things—that
those greeners had learned by God a lesson they
would never forget. They'd sure as hell never gamble
again!"

At which point Mr. Fang laughed so hard that he
knocked over the bottle of Old Overholt. Only incredibly blinding speed on the part of John Slocum
saved the moment from disaster.

"Jesus!" said Lemuel Fang, his voice round with awe, his big eyes popping out like the brass knobs on a set of hames. "I never seen such a speed! No arguing with them that says you're a fast man with a gun!"

Suddenly, what he had just said seemed to sober him, for he instantly came back to himself and a rueful and earnest look appeared on his lined, crisscrossed face. He even looked a bit sheepish, Slocum thought.

"Hell," Slocum said. "A man with your experience, Lemuel, should know by now that the hand is quicker than the eye."

This last brought the pair almost to the floor again.

But by now Slocum began to bring the conversation back onto the path he had planned it to take. Information was what he was after, information on Shiner Ratigan and Lander Miles, or for that matter, anything else that might help him.

"Tell me about Miles," he said. "I used to think he might be connected with Ratigan, but now I'm not so sure."

"No, I do believe they know each other," Fang said, suddenly quite sober. "But I don't know anything else."

And Slocum realized that the other man was staring out the alley window, and abruptly he had changed from a loquacious, cheerful individual into a guarded and closed man. Slocum now noticed the man leaning against the building across from them, but he didn't recognize him. He looked like any young drover come to town to spend his money after a drive up from Texas or after roundup work, ready to crack his nuts and wet his whistle, as the old saying had it.

But Fang's new attitude indicated that the man across the street was something more than that.

"Who is he?" he asked, as the carpenter picked up a drawknife and began working over a piece of wood in his vise.

"Dunno, Slocum. That was nice Overholt."

"Don't hand me that shit," Slocum snapped, suddenly hard. "You recognized that feller. "Who is he? One of Miles's men, one of Ratigan's?"

"I believe he's one of Ratigan's," Lemuel said, as he kept working with the drawknife. "You better watch yerself. You asked me about Miles and Ratigan. I already talked too much. The booze done it. And I want you to know right now—and I am swearing it, so help me, on a stack of Bibles—that I was just jawin' with you. There ain't a word of truth in what I said, so help me Jesus!"

Besides the back room at the Buffalo Bar that he used as an office, Shiner Ratigan had a perfectly good office in the Canham House, right alongside the hotel's restaurant, and with the advantage of easy access to any upstairs room if he had the wish or the need to stop over. Yet, for certain business he far preferred his other—a third—"office" at the far end of town in Mosman's Livery.

This establishment was possibly the oldest in Medicine Bluff, and like Burt Mosman himself had the appearance of falling apart at any moment. But also like eighty-year-old Burt, the livery hung in there. Large, drafty, rank with the smell of horse piss, manure, pack rats, leather and oil, grain, hay, and probably just plain old time, the livery remained unpainted, uncared-for, and taken for granted, relied upon always to be there. Like old Burt, that cracker-jack with his jaws forever chewing, his knobby elbows and knees, his deep-socketed eyes, stubby brown teeth, and broken-looking hands, the livery was a fixture.

It would have been impossible for anyone to figure out why Shiner Ratigan chose such a place in which to have some of his meetings. Maybe for secrecy; maybe just for a change. Old Burt allowed it was plain orneriness. But he didn't pay it much mind, as he once put it to somebody who asked him.

The "office" in question was actually a part of the tack room at the back of the huge barn, and it had been partitioned off by orders from Shriner. A stove had been put in. There was a window, through which it was impossible to see. Grime had collected over the years to such an extent that you couldn't even see the weather. There were some chairs, a table, a couple of shelves holding up a good deal of dust, plus cobwebs. The permanent residents here were the pack rats, ubiquitous in all liveries, and they didn't necessarily leave when Shiner or his associates were in the premises. Even though now and again, from irritation at their interruptions, or for simple sport and hilarity, Shiner or someone or other would engage in a little target practice. Indeed, a point was always made of Shiner's unerring aim, which pleased him.

At the moment, however, Shiner Ratigan was not

showing off his pistol prowess. It was definitely not
the moment, for his companion was none other than
Tice Finnegan, no mean pistoleer himself which was
of course why Shiner had hired him in the first place.

Both men sat in straight-backed chairs, facing
each other. Shiner was behind the desk, and Tice
alongside.

"Otis fucked up, then?" Tice was saying, his
marbley eyes on Ratigan.

"Not Otis, but that damn fool Hendry and his two
pals. Mistook Slocum for Sables. Jesus H.!"

"Didn't Otis know what the hell was goin' on?"
Tice asked, squinting at Ratigan.

"Sure he knew, but not fast enough. It all happened quicker'n a cat lickin' his own ass."

"An' this feller Slocum caught on."

"Slocum read it right with them."

"He sounds like a slicker," Tice said. "An' he
caught on to Otis?"

"Maybe he did. Thing is, he's not slow with a
gun. Thing is—"

"Dumb. Those fellers are just plain dumb!"

"Never interrupt me when I'm talking," Shiner
Ratigan snapped. And Tice Finnegan blinked.

Shiner Ratigan was red around the jowls, and he
was even madder that Tice Finnegan hadn't been
quick enough to read his sign and so had cut in on
him. Shit take it! The plan was so simple: pretend to
brace one and then when the other one's attention is
caught, you hit him coming in on his blind side. Simple! A sweetheart plan that he had thought out with
great care. And it would have stopped Sables before
he even reached Miles and his Rocking Box boys.

Otis! Yes, Otis had fucked up too. Otis should've made sure of Slocum. Only how? Never mind. He should have stopped it. He knew Slocum wasn't Sables, and the minute he got wise he should have polished Slocum off—but only so as to be sure nothing could be put at Ratigan's door.

"Otis fucked up," Tice put in now, still mad at Ratigan's dressing-down. But Shiner did not respond; he only belched softly.

"Then how you figure to correct it?" Tice Finnegan had reached deep into his pants pocket and taken out a big clasp knife and started to pare his long black nails.

"I thought maybe a shooting contest."

"I don't get you," Tice said, his eyes fully on the paring of his fingernails. "How you gonna get Sables into a shooting match? You mean—with Slocum?"

"I dunno. But we can try. Sables sees himself as top gun, and I mean with no exceptions." He looked hard at Finnegan. "But you showed a certain talent along that line. You impressed people, Tice, when you pulled off those ten bull's-eyes. Course, with a little help from Willie switching cards."

"I hit 'em all," Tice said sourly.

Shiner Ratigan smiled and said nothing.

They were both quiet for a moment, listening to a pack rat chewing at something on the other side of the wall. A horse nickered out in one of the stalls.

"Why don't you have Otis try again?"

Shiner's eyebrows lifted as he regarded the other man. "Otis had the perfect showdown. Those two kids coming in on Slocum like that. Hell, he couldn't miss. Like shooting apples in a water barrel."

"You're saying Otis should've coldcocked Slocum," Tice said, coming in smooth, careful not to interrupt. "You figure Slocum knows something?"

"I'm saying he should've killed the sonofabitch. Slocum is wise to something now, and the bastard will cause mucho trouble."

"Otis musta lost his balls," Tice said sourly. "Is he still working for us—you?" he added swiftly. "And you still want him to take care of Sables?"

"And Slocum," said Ratigan, and he clamped down hard on his cigar.

"It's easy," Tice Finnegan said, and pursed his lips, looking down at his clipped fingernails admiringly.

"Yeah?" Ratigan leaned forward. "How easy?"

Tice Finnegan's dark eyes regarded his employer benignly yet with care. "Cut their trail with a friendly Winchester, is how I sees it." And Tice leaned back, small, always dangerous, and with his tongue popping out his leathery cheek.

"Thing is," Ratigan resumed. "Thing is, I might could use the man."

"Slocum?"

"I even opened some talk with him. What the hell, he's a good man. You know, we could use some good men."

Tice started to object, but then he caught the sly smile on Shiner Ratigan's face and his eyes narrowed, then opened as his sudden understanding brought a matching smile to his own mouth and eyes, but not to the rest of him. "Keep it in the family," he said softly.

Shiner Ratigan gave a nod. "Always catch a man when he ain't looking," he said.

Tice Finnegan suddenly broke into a big grin. "By God, Shiner, I wouldn't want to try catching a man like yourself not looking!" And he let out a whoop of delighted laughter.

"That's correct," Shiner Ratigan said, his words cold enough to frost a side of beef. "That's right, you wouldn't." And his eyes were like bullets as they poked into Tice Finnegan, making that rawhide gentleman squirm in his seat.

And for several long moments they continued to sit there, each in his own chair, with Shiner Ratigan's agate eyes drilling into Tice Finnegan's leathery soul, as though he hadn't quite made up his mind whether to buy him or sell him.

In a way of speaking, things were tougher now than they'd been before the county war had settled it. So thought Lander Miles as he sat in his room in the big log ranch house staring into his crowded rolltop desk. He didn't know why he had a desk. He hadn't any need for it. After all, he did most if not all of his business in his head, or now and again on the back of a piece of bark, maybe scratching the figures with a horseshoe nail. He was for sure no bookkeeping man. His element was and always had been the saddle, not the swivel chair.

But he was older now. A tall, lean man with a cast in his left eye and a scar right nearby where a Sioux arrow had hit. Plus a few more arrow marks and a couple of bullet holes and even a scar from a knife

fight when he was a whole helluva lot younger.
Tough. Texas he was.

But now he sat there in the creaking swivel chair,
all rawhide, and in a strange way silk too. A gentleman somewhere in that hard makeup. Because he'd
long ago come from Georgia.

Tall, yes, with deep-socketed eyes, a broom mustache, and bony hands with big veins. He sat there in
the old swivel chair chewing on an unlighted cigar,
as he always did whenever he had what he called
"heavy thinking" to do.

That damn Tom Rourke! Filing on that section of
land—like behind his back. He, Miles—kind, fa-
therly Lander Miles, always looking after the best
interests of his men—had staked that damned sonofabitch so's he could file and prove up on that section, and then—as by God per agreement with
himself!—sell it back to the Rocking Box. And the
bastard had not! The bastard had kept it! Rustling
sonofabitch!

Well, he'd gotten his. The cattle war was over, but
the vigilantes hadn't quit. No, by God. Terence and
them had taken care of Rourke. Except that then that
damn son of Rourke's had done them in. And the
court done nothing to straighten it out. Not that
Lander Miles had ever been a man to rely on the
courts. Hell no. He'd always relied on his good,
swift gun hand, or a hired one. But Brom Rourke—
that damned kid!—had plumb left the country. And
that left the two girls alone. Shit! A man couldn't just
ride in and dispossess two helpless girls and get away
with it. For Miles had no scruples about getting those
damn women out of there and right now, only there

were the folks around, and in town. Two young
girls, one not even grown to womanhood yet. Well,
there were people's feelings. Mess with those two
young girls and the whole damn county would be
jumping up his ass.

And so he had to go around it. For he needed that
section of land more than ever. To close the gap in
his range. Especially now with the railroad coming
closer, and the land grabbers and sodbusters. The
range war was over, but the pitch battles were still
going on.

And of course it was a situation where he couldn't
show his hand. He had to work around things. Especially with Ratigan taking over Medicine Butte. Who
could tell how far that man would go. He had everything sewn up in town. He owned the damn place.
Well, that was all right. But it wouldn't do for him to
get cocky and think he could move out onto rangeland.

His cigar had suddenly fallen into his lap, and he
realized he needed a good smoke, so he found a lucifer in his pocket and lit up. That was better. For he
didn't like one little bit what he had heard about the
gunfight at Willow Creek stage depot. The report
that came in from his foreman, who got it straight
from the driver of the stage, was that three punks had
come gunning for Scarf Sables and had run into John
Slocum and gotten shot up and run off. And Otis
Dooley, one of Ratigan's men, had been involved.
Now why in hell had they been picking on Sables in
the first place? How had they, or anyone, even
known about Sables? And where the hell was Sables?
The man was overdue. Long overdue.

Lander Miles stood up suddenly and stretched. He looked at his Colt handgun and rigging lying in the rolltop desk, where he'd placed it before sitting down. He started to reach for the gun rig but stopped, and instead scratched himself, deep in the crotch, and suddenly thought of Maggie. His jaw tightened as he turned away from the desk, his eyes sweeping past the photograph in the silver frame that stood on top of his cigar box, which allowed the woman in the picture to look down at all his disorder —the papers, pencils, account books stuffed with more papers. And he knew how she would have scolded him, as she always had, but always funning, scolding him like he was a kid and had to be taught. He felt something behind his eyes as he walked to the big window. The window was open, and it was just getting to be dawn, and he could smell the fresh-cut hay that had been rained on during the night, and in his mind ran the thought that he would have to tell someone to turn it so it wouldn't burn. But then, no. Snow would do that. What the hell was a foreman for anyways?

He heard the heavy step on the porch, followed by the knock.

Not really wanting to be interrupted—especially when he was thinking of Maggie, remembering Maggie—he gargled out an inarticulate sound.

There was another knock.

"Come in, goddamnit! The door is open!"

It was Chuck-Charlie Snow, his ranch foreman, a man with long jaws and a hard look in his eyes. He was a good foreman who drove the men hard.

"What's going on?" his boss asked.

"Scarf Sables was in town."

"Was? Or is."

"He ain't there anymore far as I been able to find out," Chuck-Charlie said. "I got outriders watching the trails coming in. Let you know soon as he's sighted."

"Good enough."

Just then there came another knock on the door. Miles gave a slight nod to Chuck-Charlie Snow, who called out, "Come in."

It was a short, bowlegged man who entered. Most of his front teeth were missing—he was an old bronc stomper—and his hat looked like it had lived well beyond its time. Obviously it had been much used for hazing stock, slapping recalcitrant horses, and maybe too it was just old, like its owner.

Before he could speak, Miles had turned to the window, his hard back facing the two men. "Rider," Miles said, not turning from the window.

"Must be that feller Scarf somethin'," the old bronc stomper said. His name was Willie. "Harry seen him."

"Sables," said Chuck-Charlie Snow.

"He's down by the benchland," said Miles.

At a nod from Chuck-Charlie, Willie left the room.

"You want them glasses?" the foreman asked, his eyes on the field glasses on top of the rolltop desk.

"I know who it is."

The two men stood there at the window while the man on horseback approached.

"It's him, is it?" the foreman asked.

Lander Miles said nothing.

"You want some of the boys?"

"No. Let him come right in. But I want him to know he's covered. I want him to know that very well."

He was still looking out the window as his foreman left the room, closing the door firmly behind him.

Lander Miles continued to stand where he was—solid, like he was planted there—as the rider disappeared from view behind a stand of spruce. He was clearly going to follow the trail that came right up to the side of the house.

After the cattle war had ended, Miles had figured it was all over. Only it wasn't. Hell, a man had to fight for what he knew was right. He didn't like bloodshed and killing any more than the next man, but what could you do? A man couldn't just stand there picking his nose while some small stockman robbed you deaf, dumb, and blind. A man had to stand up for what was right.

He knew the rider would still be awhile, and so now he turned back into the room and walked over to his desk. He picked up his gun rigging, which he seldom wore anymore, being older and relying less on his gun hand and more on what he was and stood for with his reputation in the country and among all the cattle folk. He hefted the gun, belt, holster, and walked across the room and hung the rigging on a peg next to his Stetson hat. Then he returned to the window. The rider was still out of sight, but Lander Miles continued to stand there.

6

Leaving Lemuel Fang, Slocum slipped quickly away, avoiding the man across the street, who was obviously watching the carpentry shop. He was pretty sure he hadn't been seen—at least not leaving the premises.

He went quickly along the backs of buildings that, like Fang's shop, faced Main Street. It was getting dark now. The shadows had finished lengthening against the sides of the town and now enveloped all, only retreating at those areas where light appeared, cutting its own presence into the swiftly descending dark.

It didn't take him long to circle around and come up to the alley across the street from Fang's undertaking and carpentry shop. He couldn't see the man who was watching, but he had a feeling nonetheless that he was still there. There was a light on in the shop, and he could see Fang's stooped shadow moving about inside.

Suddenly a rider appeared on the street on a big stud horse. He'd obviously ridden in from the trail, for the animal was heated and blowing, even though the rider was walking him now, in accordance with the town law that prohibited horses being ridden fast in the dirt street and thus throwing up clouds of dust. Both horse and rider were moving along in a lively manner, nonetheless, the horse stepping quick, the man obviously watching his way with sharp attention.

He drew rein at the hitching rack in front of the Low-Hat Saloon, which was one door away from Fang's place. The rider stepped down from the big animal and, throwing a quick look up and down the street, which was fairly free of people at that time of day, started up toward the alley where Slocum had spotted the man watching Fang's place. He turned into the alley and disappeared from Slocum's view.

Slocum waited a couple of minutes and then moved down and away from the alley. After several yards he crossed over, worked his way to the back of the houses, and came up to the far end of the alley that ran next to Fang's shop, where the two men would be, unless they had moved out.

He turned the corner slowly, dropping down behind a rain barrel, and could just make out their shapes up ahead, thanks to a light that was suddenly turned on in an upstairs window in the building next to Fang's.

Yes, it looked like the man he had seen from

Fang's window, and the other he was pretty sure was the rider of the stud horse.

Slocum edged closer, taking a lot of time, keeping well down, aware that at any moment somebody could turn on a light in one of the houses that might reveal him to the two men up ahead. But he was lucky. He managed to get close enough to hear their voices, though he couldn't make out what they were saying.

Looking across, he saw Lemuel Fang moving about inside his shop. He was working with his plane again. And his body threw a big shadow on the opposite wall of his shop. The man himself was absolutely clear.

He heard the click of a hammer being pulled back, then saw the man nearest the street start to run out of the alley. He saw the outline of the remaining man lifting his gun, and Slocum's hand swept to his Colt. Two shots, almost simultaneous, almost sounding as one—but not to Slocum. He knew his had found its target, for he saw the figure drop with a cry. Then he heard the horse pounding down the street, and he saw Lemuel Fang slumping to the floor of his shop.

He ran forward. The man on the ground was dead. His companion of the moment before was galloping out of town, leaving the impression that it was he who had fired the shot. And Lemuel Fang?

Slocum raced around the building and burst in through the front door. The old man lay on the floor, bent almost double, but still alive.

He was trying to curse, but the pain was obviously too great for him to say the words.

Slocum knelt down beside him, holstering his

gun. "Take it easy, old-timer. Help'll be here in a minute. I think I got the sonofabitch for you."

Lemuel Fang stared blindly at Slocum through his pain. He'd been hit high in the chest, and there was already a lot of blood. Slocum had just started to cut away the old man's shirt, using his clasp knife, when the men pounded in behind him.

"Slocum, you're under arrest! Throw up your hands!" It was Otis Dooley speaking, and the marshal's badge was pinned firmly to his faded blue shirt. He was accompanied by Chet Sindall, the man who had been deputy under Felix Horne, and Tice Finnegan.

"I didn't shoot him," Slocum said. "You'll find the killer out in the alley."

Otis Dooley turned to the men who had burst into the shop with him. "Tice, you go see if there's anybody out in the alley."

And with a sinking feeling Slocum knew the answer to that one well before Tice Finnegan returned to tell the new marshal that there wasn't anybody out in the alley. "Not anybody—alive or dead."

"What about that horse galloping out of town?" Slocum said, making one last and, he knew, futile stab at it.

"Mister, you got air in your head. Now we'll just head down to my new office, and your new home, which is right behind it." Otis looked down at the bleeding Lemuel Fang, who seemed in slightly less pain, though still hurting plenty. "If that man dies— and he sure might—I'll be charging you with murder."

• • •

It took Slocum all of maybe five minutes to discover that there was no way out of the log structure that served as the jail in Medicine Butte. A small one-story building built solid as a tomb out of straight, even spruce with the bark left on, with one door and no window and not much air. Thanks to the solidity of the carpentry, there wasn't even a draft allowed through the chinking. Slocum wondered if maybe Lem Fang had built the little fort. But such speculation did nothing to mitigate his dismay at being incarcerated.

Lemuel Fang, he'd been told, was still hovering between life and death.

Otis Dooley made it painfully clear that even if Lem survived, Slocum would still stand trial for "attempted murder."

Slocum gave his own statement of innocence, telling what actually had happened, and then remained silent. When questioned again by Dooley, and also by Tice Finnegan and Chet Sindall, his deputies, Slocum simply said that he had told all he knew and that they could take it or leave it. He wasn't going to play their damn game.

"You'll get a fair trial, Slocum," Otis said heavily. He was standing in front of his prisoner, who was seated on his bunk, the sole piece of furniture in the log jail.

"I know I can't go broke betting on that," Slocum commented drily.

"And you ain't got a prayer of excapin'." Otis's big head tilted as his eyes went to the roof and roamed over the log walls, "Even with outside help,

I'd say you'd about as much chance as a one-armed man busting a calf in a Kansas twister."

"Anything else?" Slocum said.

"Yeah, there is," Otis canted his head and looked slowly at his prisoner. "You, uh, got company."

"Company? I don't know anybody in this town." He could think of nobody who might visit him under the present circumstances. The thought of Shiner Ratigan did enter his mind, though for no special reason, but it passed.

"I'll send her in," Otis said with a sly smile that made Slocum want to hit him. "Remember, any wrong move and you're both done for."

It was Ginny, the barber-bath girl, and Slocum was delighted to see her.

"Surprised?" Her smile was broad, but he detected a trace of tension in her eyes and the corners of her mouth. At the same time, she looked better than ever, and he was at once caught up in her aroma, her sensual movements as she sat down on the edge of his bunk, the way she crossed her legs. Even so, Slocum was keeping his attention on the main event —escape.

"They sent you, did they," he said. It was a statement, not at all a question. "So what do they want, as if I didn't know."

She reached up and brushed her hair back from her eyes and smiled at him, her eyes on his mouth. Then she caught herself and straightened her back, uncrossed her legs, and sat with her knees firmly together. "They did talk to me. Two men. I dunno who they were. They came up to my room. They said someone had sent them, and that I was to tell you somebody would visit you in the jail here, and you had to do what they said, or . . . or somebody would get hurt." And her mouth began to work, yet she didn't cry. She didn't even release a sound. She sat very still, staring across at the log wall.

"What are you thinking?" he asked. "Are you scared?"

"Yeh, I'm scared. But what was I thinking? I was thinking how I want to go to bed with you."

All at once she burst into tears. She shook, she sobbed, the tears cascaded down her cheeks, her makeup running with it in one massive flow.

He put his arm around her shoulders to comfort her. And after a moment or so her trembling stopped.

"Can we do it, Slocum? I want you like I never wanted anybody."

"Sure," he said. "But not here."

"Where then?"

"We'll have to wait till I get out."

"But it's private here. God, this is the most private place I was ever in. Who's ever going to bother us here?"

"That feller who just moved that chinking between those logs on that wall behind you. Don't turn around."

"You mean there's somebody watching?"

"Why do you think they let you in here?"

"Holy Moses! Some men are liable to do anything."

"Some women, too, don't forget. Did they search you when you came in?"

"Yeah, and they told me if I did anything wrong, or you did, that they'd beat me." Her face twisted again in fear. "They said they'd cut me. Slocum, who are they?"

"I'm not sure. But look, do you want to help me? I mean, I'll look after you, though I can't promise anything."

"Slocum, I'll help you any way I can. I don't want to get beat up, though."

"That I can't guarantee, that they won't beat you, but I can promise you that if they do they'll have to settle with me."

She was looking at him with longing, but with more than just that. There was something there that touched him.

"Tell me what to do," she said. "I want to help you get out of here."

Suddenly there came the sound of someone at the door, and the rattle of keys.

"Come back after dark," he whispered. "Bring me a gun barrel. Hide it under your clothes."

"A gun!"

"Only the barrel, or a piece of heavy pipe. Pipe is better. For a club," he added as the door opened and Otis Dooley walked in.

"That's enough," Dooley said.

She threw Slocum a shy smile, hidden from Dooley, who stood there with his hand on his gun.

"Don't try anything, Slocum," Dooley said.

"I wouldn't think of it."

But Slocum had heard another slight movement outside the cabin door, and knew that Dooley was backed by another gun.

No, he wouldn't try anything. Not right now.

Especially since he knew that that was exactly what they wanted him to do.

This had been one of the hottest days in a while, the sun burning into the land, going deep down to the grass roots, heating the earth, the rocks, the trees. The mighty sun was everywhere—at the edge of town porches, on the wooden boardwalks blistering the bare feet of children who went without their shoes. It pressed into the houses, it drew the reeking smell of horse urine and droppings from the street, it burned.

And it had burned his shoulders all the way out of town and on the long ride up to the North Fork and the trail leading deep into the Rocking Box range.

He knew that his black shirt, black pants, and black hat with the hard brim drew extra heat, but he accepted it. He had always worn black. He didn't know why, and the question had never come up for him. It was simply so, and it had always been so.

And he accepted the heat. He knew that heat kept his limbs loose, that he could draw and shoot faster in hot weather. He knew too how a man had to be aware of every advantage, every inch that he could get. It was all in that inch, in the balance, in the concentration.

He wore a black silk bandanna around his neck. Some said that was how he got the name Scarf. Others said they didn't know how he got named that way. And there were surely some who didn't think about it one way or the other. Anyway, a lot of names were summer names in that big country. No one asked questions about a man's history. There were things a man didn't need to know about another man, and things he didn't want to know. A man kept his nose clean that way. Scarf Sables was one of those. He kept his nose clean. He did his business, and he got paid for what he did. He did whatever he did well. He could have said, had he ever wanted to, that no customer had ever brought any complaint against him.

His horse was a big buckskin stud, lion-colored, with a black mane and a black line running down his long back to his black tail.

Sables had spotted the outriders early, and he knew right away that they wanted him to see them. He read from this something of the character of the man named Lander Miles. It was the first draw from the new pack, and the man known as Scarf Sables knew that Lander Miles was playing his cards strong and real close to his vest. He admired that. He admired a strong man who knew just what he wanted. For it was the weak ones you had to be careful with. you could always count on a strong man, especially if he was an enemy. But a weak man could do anything, and it would inevitably be something leading to big trouble.

He spotted another outrider now, off to his right, just a short distance from the Rocking Box, and then yet another, off to his left. Quite a crowd. There were probably more out of sight.

He didn't care. He didn't give a damn. He was not moved by this obvious display of power. Hell, the big man always fell harder than the little. Any damn fool knew that. Mr. Colonel Colt was the Great

Equalizer. And he was always fair. He played no favorites.

Sables rode up the long coulee now and came right onto the Rocking Box. As he came into view of the ranch buildings and corrals, six riders began to close in on him. They'd been riding with him all along, but at a distance. Now they formed themselves into a close escort. Yet they were not aggressive, they weren't trying to scare him, he knew. They were only trying to impress him. And failing. The fools.

At this point more men came out of the big barn and the bunkhouse. All told there were about a dozen Rocking Box men as he rode right up to the big house and sat his big buckskin horse quietly, letting his cool eyes rove around the faces of the men in front of him, feeling the presence of those behind. Now he swung around suddenly in his saddle and searched the group to his rear.

"Help you, mister?"

He swung back to look directly at the speaker.

"I'm here to see Lander Miles."

"What's the name, mister?"

The man in black didn't answer.

"Mister, what's your name?"

Scarf Sables didn't look at the speaker. He held out his right hand just a little in front of him and looked down at it, then rubbed it lightly with his left. He was wearing black leather gloves.

Still without looking at anyone he said, "You tell Miles I'm here. And tell him right now."

• • •

It was common knowledge, or at least gossip, how Shiner Ratigan had laid the foundation for a hefty fortune in the shovel trade up around Alder Gulch. Shiner had simply bought up and imported as much of a shovel supply as he could get, then started a stampede by sending riders out waving bags of dust and screaming at the top of their lungs, "Gold! Gold at Alder Gulch and half a dozen other places!"

It was only natural that people would listen to and follow a man who showed such initiative and enterprise.

When he had first arrived in Medicine Butte, only hours after his arrival, he had stopped a lynching, set up a court and tried the accused, and established law and order, and not so incidentally had himself elected chief constable. From then on he rode the wave to high political and social—not to forget monetary—office. He imported a member of the clergy, Reverend Josiah Baynes, to handle church matters, as well as a couple of schoolteachers, a lawyer, and a banker. Reverend Josiah Baynes—known formerly as Jersey Joe Baynes, a retired pugilist with more losses than wins to his credit—soon built his flock into a well-paying, respectable congregation. He ran charities, games, dances for the young and the elderly, always with the proceeds going toward "the benefit of the Lord."

It wasn't long before Medicine Butte belonged to Shiner Ratigan "both ways from the jack." As Lander Miles was quick to note, it was inevitable— and both Miles and Ratigan foresaw it—that these two men would lock horns.

Miles was trying to consolidate his holdings following the "victory" of the small stockmen in the cattle war—a victory that they were in the process of losing to their adversaries, the big stockgrowers—and was ill prepared for the unexpected spread of the Ratigan enterprise into rangeland. In short, Ratigan, through various other dummy companies and private persons, was buying up land from sodbusters and small cattlemen who had gone broke under the offensives of the big stockgrowers and their association.

It was a bitter pill to swallow. And Miles was not going to swallow it.

"It is we, the stockmen, who have worked the cattle and the land and built this western country. It is we who have held back the encroachments, the thievery and rustling, the damn spreading of the nesters, the sodbusters, the rustlers. And by God we are not about to suddenly let this sonofabitch snake-oil merchant slide in and nick the results of our hard-earned labor."

His speech at the Stock Club in Laramie brought the crowd of ranchers and stockgrowers to their feet with a mighty cheer. Indeed, it was a great speech. So the daily paper said, and so everyone who was anyone agreed.

But before you could whistle "Dixie," this patent-medicine hawker, this swindler, sharp, and con man had cut into the range country surrounding Medicine Butte and moreover had established the whole law-and-order procedure in Medicine Butte and Buffalo County. All done behind the backs of those hard-working, patriotic men who were carving the Great American West out of the wild wilderness of the savages and relentless nature.

Lander Miles was a God-fearing, honest man—
honest as the day was long—and law-abiding. But
Ratigan and his gang of sharps and shills, steerers
and fleecers, were anything but open and above-
board. And by a long shot. Yes, the stockmen had
had to be tough. After all, it had all been for proper
and noble ends, the cattle war. Yes, even what happened to Rourke. But this was a man's country, and
if you weren't tough enough you went under. Rourke
had gone under. And his prize piece of land was staring them all right in the face. Lander Miles knew it
had also to be staring Ratigan in the face.

It had been no trouble at all for Lander to convince his fellow stockmen that his plan was the only
possible way to go. Things had already gone far
enough, and now stern measures were required.

He had convinced them. And they had cheered
him. Now it was time for action.

Lander Miles was thinking of all this; he was seeing the picture, the large picture, within which the
details would be precisely worked out. The large picture was to take the Double R and mop up all the
loose, available land in the Lazy Water Valley and
environs for good measure, for extra protection. But
the main strike was the Rourke spread, it was the
very axis of the plan. This was the picture he had
shown them and to which they had all agreed with
high enthusiasm.

The precise, the acute picture was simple, incredibly simple, and always brought a somewhat hard
smile to his face as he thought of it. It did now as he
looked at the precise man sitting in the chair only a
few feet away from him.

"Good you finally got here," Lander Miles said as he lifted his glass of whiskey. His visitor lifted his, and both drank.

"What is it you want, Mr. Miles?" Scarf Sables asked. "My gun is for hire. My life is at risk. Beyond that—if there is anything—it is my own."

It had been good seeing Ginny, though somewhat difficult in view of the fact that he had suddenly felt extremely horny for her, as obviously she had been for him. Well, that was the way it went. In any case, the visit had charged him, and he had come up with a plan of escape. For he could see that he'd been set up by Ratigan. Ratigan wanted something, probably his gun, and now he could put the squeeze to him.

But who had shot Lem Fang? Was it Ratigan's men? Had someone gotten the idea that Fang was talking to Slocum? It seemed so.

But where did Miles's Rocking Box fit into the picture? And the Rourkes? He decided right now that as soon as he got out he'd ride for the North Fork to see those two lovely girls. For suddenly he had a strong feeling that they were either in danger right now or going to be in it pretty soon. The move by Ratigan—putting him in jail—was obviously the beginning of a whole new play.

He didn't have long to wait to see which way things were going. Ginny had been gone hardly a half hour when he heard the key in the door lock, voices, and then the door swung open and in walked Otis Dooley, preceding a beaming Shiner Ratigan, followed by two sallow-faced gents with low-slung hardware on their hips.

They were hardly inside the cabin when Shiner turned, still smiling amiably, and said, "You two can wait outside, I think. And you too, Otis."

All three showed their surprise, but carefully, as they turned and went back outside. Otis closed the door at a nod from Ratigan.

"Well, Slocum, I am indeed sorry for this little, uh, misunderstanding. Of course, there's no question in my mind that you are innocent of shooting old Lem Fang. But Otis is the law, after all, and he is a stickler." He had seated himself on a corner of the cot, nodding to Slocum to take the other corner. But Slocum walked across the cabin to the wall and hunkered down. It was a good distance for communication, and also to watch all the expressions and giveaways in Shiner Ratigan's speech and movement. It was always best, Slocum knew, to watch a man when he was talking to you, and much easier to read what he was really saying.

"I do hope you're not feeling leery of me, Slocum. Hope you don't think I had anything to do with your being locked up." The smile was easy and well oiled, and of course the purveyor of all that grease undoubtedly intended just the opposite—that Slocum would assuredly know that Ratigan had planned the whole episode and was now building up to a deal that he would offer as payment for his prisoner's freedom.

"It's your move, Ratigan. I'm just here for the hayride."

Shiner Ratigan beamed all over his carved face, but he didn't allow any of it into his eyes. Those agates revealed not the slightest luminosity; they were simply cold windows out of which their owner stared at the man hunkered down beside the door of his prison.

"You know a man name of Sables? Scarf Sables?" Ratigan asked suddenly.

"Don't know the gent, but I've heard of him," Slocum said, taking a quirly out of his pocket. He reached inside his belt and brought out a lucifer and struck it, smiling a tight smile as he saw the surprise in Ratigan's face.

"They didn't do such a good job cleaning you out, did they?"

"Don't look so," Slocum said, speaking around the quirly as he lighted it. "I been meaning to speak to you about the poor help you've got in your outfit."

"My outfit?"

"Medicine Butte. It's your outfit, ain't it?"

"That depends on which way a man is looking."

"Let's say he's looking into the business end of a .45."

Ratigan chuckled. "I like your humor, Slocum. But I want to hear what you think of Scarf Sables."

"That information will cost you."

"What?"

Slocum jerked his thumb toward the door. "I'll talk to you when I'm out of here."

Ratigan seemed to hesitate, but only for a second or two, and then he was up and had walked to the door and hit it twice with his fist. "Otis!"

There was the rattle of keys and then the key pushing into the lock.

Slocum was quick to see how Ratigan stepped away from the door, a very quick sidestepping, as though he knew what was going to happen even as the door burst open and Otis Dooley and the two gunmen swept in past him.

"You want to see who's running this town, Slocum?" snapped the gambler.

The two gunmen charged like a single battering ram, while Otis Dooley lifted his handgun to pistol-whip Slocum.

Only Slocum wasn't there. He had anticipated Ratigan's trick at the last second, realizing the man had agreed much too quickly to his proposition.

Sidestepping the double battering ram, he kicked Otis in the chin and slammed his fist into the pit of his big belly, knocking the wind completely out of him. Then, as the two gunmen charged again, he dropped to a crouching position, placed the palms of his hands together to make a wedge, and smashed one of them in the crotch. The man let out a scream of pain, toppling against his companion, whom Slocum now smashed in the kidney with his fist. The man screamed, staggered, fell.

But now Slocum found himself brought to the floor as Shiner Ratigan grabbed him around the knees. Then they were all over him. A fist hit him in the face, he was kicked, pummeled, yanked to his feet, and held with his arm pulled up behind his back in a hammerlock.

Shiner Ratigan's face was inches from his. The man was livid, shaking with fury. "I see they taught you well in Quantrill's band, Slocum. But by God, that won't help you any right now."

Suddenly, Slocum let himself go totally limp, his knees buckling as he slid toward the floor. In surprise his captors' grip loosened, and reaching down he grabbed one around the ankle, pulled, drove his elbow backward into somebody's crotch, then was smashed in turn by a fist that felt as though it had broken his spine. He fell to the floor, and they piled on him. Or, at any rate, two did. Otis Dooley was out of it, and Ratigan stood wheezing to one side, his gun drawn as he looked for an opening where he could use the barrel.

Somehow, even with the two gunmen on top of him, Slocum managed to free himself and struggled to his feet, elbowing one across the bridge of his nose. The man screamed with pain, and blood gushed. His companion charged Slocum, but fell over the prone Otis Dooley, who was sighing with pain on the floor.

Slocum, charged suddenly with a new force as he saw his opportunity, smashing the gun out of Ratigan's hand, and he half fell, half ran through the door.

It was only a few steps from the jail to the rear of the marshal's office. And he made it, as Shiner Ratigan recovered his .45 and fired wildly after him.

Slocum ran through the back door of the office and was suddenly confronted by the sight of Ginny holding something wrapped in a towel. She had obviously just come in from the street. Without saying a word, she pulled away the towel and handed Slocum the hard steel gun barrel he'd asked for. Then, to his astonishment, she reached up and ripped open the bodice of her dress, pulling it open all the way down to her wàist, revealing a holstered Colt .45 tied just beneath her copious white breasts, the nipples of which—Slocum always remembered this great detail—were as hard as the gun barrel she had handed him, and the .45 he now snatched from the holster.

He spun now just as the two gunmen charged into the office, throwing lead as they came. The next few minutes filled the room with gunsmoke, noise, and cursing. When the smoke cleared, one gunman lay dead and his companion was folded over the marshal's desk with a bullet in his thigh, yet alive. The girl was standing in the middle of the room, holding her dress together, her eyes staring at the carnage, frightened yet not terrified, looking as though she had no notion of what to do or how to be, and so she had accepted to be just whatever she was right then and there.

"I am unarmed, Slocum," Shiner Ratigan called through the open door. "I want to come in and talk to you. But I want you to know I am unarmed."

"And alone," Slocum said. "You come in alone. Where's Otis?"

"He's wounded. He's out in the cabin."

"Come in, then," Slocum said. "But one funny move from you or anybody else and you're dead."

A white-faced Shiner Ratigan walked in slowly. Yet he was calm and collected, and the color was already returning to his face. His eyes slowly swept the room. "Ginny, go get a doctor," he said.

Slocum nodded as the girl turned her eyes to him. "If anything happens to her, Ratigan, I won't kill you, I'll burn the hide off you—slowly."

"I guess you really did ride with Quantrill, my lad."

Slocum drew back the hammer of the Colt he was

holding in his right hand. "That will be enough of that," he said.

And Ulysses "Shiner" Ratigan sighed, as though his good humor had returned.

"I own this town, Slocum. You won this round—with some help, I have to add. And I could have you wiped out within five minutes. Excepting I want you to help me. Like I said, I could use a good man."

"I know you need me, Ratigan. Especially with a man like Sables maybe working against you, eh?"

"That's why I asked you about him."

"He is working for"—and here Slocum took a wild plunge as he said—"Miles, I'll allow."

He saw that he had scored, even though Ratigan remained silent.

Slowly, Slocum holstered his six-gun, keeping his eyes carefully on Ratigan as he did so. "Thing is, Ratigan, while you've got a reason for wanting me, I don't know any reason for me wanting you."

"Oh, I do, Slocum. I do." And the smile that came into those agate eyes was as sly as a coyote. "I know a good reason."

Slocum said nothing, for he suddenly knew the answer to that, and he felt the ice gripping him in his guts.

"You have forgotten your two young friends, Slocum. But I assure you, Lander Miles has not forgotten them. Nor have I."

Slocum heard the footsteps outside the door.

"Come in, boys. But no shooting. Slocum here is going to be working with us, and so I want you to offer him every courtesy. Meaning you never let him out of your sight."

As he was saying these words, the men came filing in, a half dozen in all. All were heavily armed, and all looked impassively at the smashed office and the two adversaries who stood there.

"He'll keep his gun," Ratigan said. "Any man working for Shiner Ratigan has to have a gun."

7

In the early morning a light mist had enveloped the valley, hiding the river and indeed the sweeping land all the way down to the ranches halfway to Medicine Butte. Seen from the Rourke spread the belt of mist covered the Z-Bar, the Quarter Circle HO, and the Four-Dot, but not the Rocking Box, which was higher up and across the valley.

Nellie and Caney Rourke had started their washing early, and by halfway through the forenoon they had everything hung on lines for drying.

Nellie always liked doing the wash. She liked the feel of the suds as she worked the linen in the galvanized tub. She liked the steaming hot water, heated on the kitchen range. And she loved the smell of the flannel sheets after they'd dried in the mountain wind and she was folding them.

Meanwhile Caney was putting up stock in her

mason jars for the coming winter. The root cellar in back of the cabin, dug into the high bank of the mountain leading up to the rimrocks, already had a supply of game, beans, rutabagas, hominy, and spuds. At the same time, she was baking biscuits in the oven for present use.

Caney looked up, her eyes going to the window across from the kitchen range, through which she could see her sister pinning laundry to the line that she'd strung between the corner of the cabin and a pole. She watched the long, wide sheets curling as the wind licked at the laundry, flapping a couple of shirts, snapping the already drying overalls, and with a sudden gust, whipping the support pole over to its other side and almost spilling the wash.

Outside, Nellie had heard the horse coming up the trail through the tall timber. Looking quickly toward the corral, through which anyone approaching would have to pass, she wondered if she should get into the house. But suddenly her attention was caught by the beauty of the scene below. The mist had suddenly cleared, and the sun was shining gloriously over the green and brown land all the way down to the Z-Bar, or what had been the Z-Bar before somebody—she wasn't sure who—had bought it up from old Jesse Linctus.

She was again watching the opening to the trail through the stand of spruce through which the rider would appear when she heard the voice behind her.

"I see my partner an' me timed it just right, miss. Riding in together like."

Nellie felt something pumping hard inside her, even though her breath seemed to stop at the same

time. But she was a brave girl; she was a Rourke.
And so she was quiet and well inside herself when
she turned and faced the tall, thin man in the black
shirt and pants, the black hat, and black gloves.

"So it was those two who tried to drygulch me out by
Butler Pass," Slocum was saying as he sat facing
Shiner Ratigan. "I do believe they had a couple of
other rattlers with them." He grinned savagely at his
captor, who was smoking a cigar. "Pretty piss-poor
bunch if you ask me, which you weren't, but I'm
telling it anyways."

"They weren't trying to kill you, Slocum. Just
wanted to persuade you a little." Ratigan chuckled
mirthlessly. "But it comes up that you're a hard man
to persuade. Howsomever, there are ways, my
friend."

"I heard you the first time, Ratigan. And I promise you one thing. If anything happens to either of
those Rourke girls, what I will do to you and your
buddies here will make Lawrence look like a game of
pattycake."

Shiner Ratigan's agate eyes lighted up. "You were
at Lawrence, Slocum, were you? I know you rode
with Quantrill. Taught you some bad manners, that
man did."

"Mister, I never had to ride with Quantrill or
Bloody Bill Anderson or anyone else to know what
to do with scum like your two there." He nodded
toward the two gunmen, each squatting in a separate
corner of the room, with their handguns drawn. "Interesting," Slocum went on. "Here I am, unarmed,
and those little buggers are afraid to keep their pop

pistols holstered." He grinned. "Or is it you who's afraid, Ratigan?"

Ratigan suddenly leaned forward on his knees. "You know, Slocum, I could have them kill you right now."

"I know."

"I could have them tie you up and torture you."

"Sure you could."

With each of Shiner Ratigan's statements Slocum's words shot back at him like a battering ram.

For a moment Ratigan was nonplussed. He stared hard at his prisoner. "You know, Slocum," he said slowly. "You know something. I do believe you mean it."

Slocum said nothing.

"What I'm saying is I do believe you don't give a damn. Like, you got no holes in you. You don't bend, you don't dent, you don't give. For Chrissake, you're worse'n a fuckin' Indian. What the hell you made of?"

"You figure that out."

"You don't give a damn whether you live or die, do you?"

Slocum's green eyes were cold and hard as marble as he looked directly at Shiner Ratigan. "I sure do give a damn, Ratigan. That's why I know how I'm going to die."

Ratigan's eyebrows shot up. "How the hell can you know that, fer Chrissakes! Nobody knows how he's gonna die."

"I do."

Shiner Ratigan was suddenly sweating. "How?" he said. "Tell me. I want to know. I want to know," he added, and clamped his jaws together tight.

Slocum looked at Ratigan's hands. The gambler was holding them together tight. Very tight.

"It's easy," Slocum said softly. "To figure how I'm going to die just means I got to know how I'm *not* going to die. See?" His eyes were still boring into the other man.

"How? How you figure you're not gonna die. How d'you know about it, like ahead. How you're gonna die, or not gonna die—whatever. By God, I want to know. You tell me! I want you to tell me!"

A hard grin cut into Slocum's mouth, then reached his eyes. "How I'm not going to die is like a pimp. I'm not going to die like you."

He watched the other man's fingers twitch, waiting for him to go for his gun, ready to dive low and to the side, and keeping Ratigan between himself and the two gunmen by the door.

But Shiner Ratigan held his fire. His hand clenched into a fist, his mouth became a straight line. He sat rigid in his chair, his eyes burning into the man opposite him.

"We'll see about that, Slocum. We'll see when the time comes. Meanwhile, there are the girls. I think you understand what I'm saying to you. There are the Rourke young ladies."

"I told you what I'll do if anything happens to them, Ratigan. Nothing, you understand? Nothing must happen to them. You understand me?"

"I hear you, my friend. But this is not a Mexican standoff. You have something I want. And I have something you want."

"Potentially," Slocum said. "You are speaking of

the possibilities of what we can give each other." He was watching Ratigan closely. He had seen immediately the whitening of the other's lips and eyes as he'd said the word "pimp." At the same time, he realized the foolishness of standing on his line and not negotiating. He had to deal with the man. Even though Ratigan didn't have his hands on the Rourkes, he could easily get them. And so it made sense to go along with him. Of course, only so far.

"There is also another, uh, point," Shiner Ratigan said, looking sideways at Slocum.

"And that is?"

"That is a, uh, friend of yours." Ratigan's smile was sly, his lower lip, wet and with a fleck of tobacco on it, hung down. His eyes bore into Slocum.

"I didn't know I had any friends in Medicine Butte."

"There is Lemuel Fang. He's a friend, isn't he? I am happy to say he has survived his, uh, recent passage at arms."

"I see." Although for the moment, he didn't. And then suddenly he realized what Ratigan was getting at, and another savage twist of apprehension ran through his whole body.

"There is, too, your friend Ginny. You wouldn't want anything to happen to Ginny, now would you?"

"Nor would you!" Slocum snapped, sharp as a knife. "Just remember that, Ratigan." He stood up. "Tell me what you want, then," he said, looking down at the gambler.

Shiner Ratigan had his full attention on Slocum

now. "I want you to kill Scarf Sables," he said. "And maybe also Lander Miles."

"I want you to kill John Slocum."

These words, bulleting out of the hard mouth of that veteran of the trail and frontier, Lander Miles, reached the awareness of the man in black with instant recognition of the task ahead.

Scarf Sables nodded. "The man has needed killing this good while," he said, his voice soft, the words couched in promise.

"I don't care how you do it so long as it doesn't have anything to do with the Rocking Box."

"Or yourself, I'll allow."

"That is correct," Miles said, his voice hard as a fist.

A silence fell. It was their second meeting, this one following Sables' visit to the Rourke spread and his encounter with Nellie and Caney Rourke.

"Now tell me what happened at the Double R," Miles said.

Scarf Sables accepted the cigar the rancher offered, and while he bit off the little bullet of tobacco at the end and lighted up, he said nothing. He kept his eyes on his host, who was going through the same performance. In a moment the office at the Rocking Box ranch was hazy with large pillows of cigar smoke.

"She's a cute little thing," Sables said.

"I didn't send you there for that," snapped Miles.

Suddenly Sables chuckled. But there was no mirth in it. His teeth shone—they were shiny and false—

but he was not laughing at all. His laughter had been at Miles's weakness. The weakness of other men always amused Scarf Sables.

"And so is her younger sister," the man in black went on, enjoying fully the anger and alarm he had stirred in the rancher.

"Tell me what you did, how they were, what they said."

"I just told 'em what we spoke about, you an' me. Said I was interested in buyin' the place. Said I knew you wanted it too, and you'd made an offer, but here I was makin' a bigger, better offer. And how I figured by now she an' her sister had thought it over and were more sensible about selling."

"You let her know you were working for me?"

"I let her know I was working *with* you," Sables said, coming down hard on the "with."

Lander Miles belched suddenly. He had always been able to belch at will, ever since he was a small boy, and had even won fame in school for this ability. He belched now, and as always it was his way of signaling disapproval, disgust.

"But I didn't let her know direct," Sables went on, and his lean face, Miles thought, looked more pinched and like a hungry coyote than ever.

"Good, then. They'll feel the pressure. Who did you take along with you?"

"Dunstan."

"There are two Dunstans. Which one?"

"The feller with the harelip."

"How was he?"

"He done what I told him. Exceptin', like most of

your hands, he ain't worth much more'n a fart in a snowbank."

"The boys," Lander Miles said, "are not professional gunmen, Sables, like yourself. They are not killers. They are trail hands, they know how to handle horses and cattle. They ain't gun hawks. But don't deal them from the bottom of the deck." He leaned forward suddenly. "Know something? I wouldn't trade a pair of my hands for a pair of any other kind of man I know of. Not that I wouldn't tear the shit out of any one of them that loused up his job."

"Well, well. Good for you, then," said Scarf Sables, and the sneer wasn't only in his voice, it was all over his face.

"I'm telling you that those men are solid. Give or take here and there, you take any man what's ridden the cattle drag up from Texas, has handled a stampede, storm, not to mention some of those unfriendly Injuns, by God you got a man to ride the river with. But now, nowadays . . ." He let it hang, and drew on his cigar while a stiff silence entered the room.

After a moment Sables said, "You want to pay me somethin' on account, Miles?" He stood up.

"No," Lander Miles said. "No. I pay on delivery." And he stood up and faced the gunman. "That was our original agreement, and that's what we'll stick by."

As he left the room there was a tight grin on Scarf Sables' face. He had only been testing the rancher. He'd only wanted to see how far he could push. Not very far. But it was good. He liked working with a

man like Lander Miles. You knew where you stood
with such a man.

Lemuel Fang sat on the three-legged stool, regarding
the half-finished coffin he'd been working on when
he'd been shot. Lucky, he was thinking. Lucky it
hadn't been he'd been building it for himself. He
wondered who had shot him. Could be someone
from Ratigan's rat crew, as he called it to himself, or
maybe one of Lander Miles's bunch. Or—not likely,
by God—somebody from before, from the past,
looking to get even on something or other. Maybe
even something he himself had long forgotten about.

There was no point in studying it too long. Ru-
minating on it only got you in a mess. Lemuel was a
man who understood philosophy. And he knew he
had to save himself. There were tough times a-
comin', and he'd have to be ready. He stood up now
and walked slowly toward the carpenter's bench that
ran along part of one wall. He checked the blade on
the plane, and carried it to the unfinished coffin.
Felix had to be pretty stiff by now, he told himself,
laying in that icehouse all that time since Burke
Tobin had shot him. Well, he'd be planted soon
enough. Day after tomorrow, they'd told him. Be a
ceremony, and like that. Hell, Felix Horne wasn't
just any old stiff in the bone orchard. He was a
United States marshal, by God; had been, that is.
Lem was humming to himself as he moved the plane
across the pine wood, and he didn't hear the step
behind him.

"How-do, Lem," the voice said.

And Lem Fang felt his guts twist as he straightened up, and turned slowly to face his visitor.

He stood there in his carpenter shop, looking right at the man in black. And for an instant there, there had been that fear slicing through him as he'd heard the familiar voice. The fear he'd lived with a long time, from before Medicine Butte, from way back— way back all the way to Lead Town.

"Long time," Sables said.

"Not long enough," Lem replied. And as he spoke he felt that surge in him of something. It was like a spring that he'd known long ago and that was suddenly released after a forever time of being muzzled, with only a trickle coming through. But now. . . And now. . .

"Had no notion you was in Medicine Butte," Sables was saying, a nasty smile playing about his mouth, while his dark eyes darted like twin snakeheads.

"What you want?" Lem said, picking up a splinter of wood and using it as a toothpick.

Suddenly he had never felt so good in his life. He wanted to laugh. He didn't try to understand it. After all these years. After all these years of fear, hiding, yes—terror. And here the sonofabitch was. Standing there, real close. Well, go ahead, you fourteen-karat prick. Go ahead!

"Go ahead, Sables," he said. "You want me to turn my back first? That make it easier for you?"

Lemuel Fang picked up his plane and began working on the coffin. His eyes, his whole attention—except for the part that was on his visitor—was on his work. Only those two things. He was totally concentrated as Scarf Sables' hand dropped to his gun butt.

He worked, waiting.

Then Sables spoke. "You're different, Lemuel."

"You aren't," Lem said without looking up from his work. And now to his own astonishment he stopped for a moment, ran his hand along the part he had planed, then turned his back to the man in black —the man from his past—and began planing the board from the other end, with his back turned toward Scarf Sables, whose right hand was still on the grip of his holstered Colt .45.

For a moment he waited for the click, the shot, the blow, whatever. His body was tense, though not shaking, and to his further amazement, he realized he wasn't trembling. Not even a quiver was running through him. And yet he wasn't blocked off. He was right there, yet calm, cool, collected. He could have held a small bird in the palm of his hand, he told himself. And for a moment he again wanted to laugh.

The moment was not endless. It was simply what it was, and Lem didn't think of it in any way of measuring. It was what it was. It was a good moment.

Scarf Sable's voice was almost a whisper. "I don't believe I got any reason to kill you again, Lemuel."

Lem Fang stopped planing the piece of wood. His thoughts continued, though, as he ran his hand over the surface. Then, bending, he eyeballed the work for trueness. It was right, it ought to join right well with the corner. Felix Horne was going to have a good coffin to lie in. By God, a damn good coffin.

He straightened, though not all the way, on account of he was actually for a fact seventy-some pushing on eighty. And his eyes went to the sign that was nailed above the door to his carpenter shop, and which he had brought with him from way back, way back to the old days in Lead Town: "Within these portals man finds his last abode—Lemuel Fang, Builder of Coffins."

Ratigan had let him go, as Slocum knew he would. He was no good to the gambler dead. Somehow Ratigan had decided he could use him. Or maybe it was that another killing in town at this particular moment would have been troublesome, might have drawn unnecessary attention into areas which Ratigan would rather have kept out of sight. Hell, it didn't matter. He was alive.

He realized now that he was being followed. Well, that was to be expected. Ratigan surely wanted to know what his "prisoner" was up to, and he would also exert pressure on his gunning down Scarf Sables.

"See you're still about," Highpockets Purdy observed conversationally as he poured a shot for Slocum at the Buffalo Bar.

"Didn't you expect it?"

Highpockets looked like he had suddenly forgotten something at that point, and slid down to the other end of the bar, holding his bar rag as he went and making a wide swathe past the glasses and bottles and elbows.

"I expected it," the voice said behind Slocum, and Slocum smiled into the big mirror in front of him in which Ginny was smiling back at him.

"Fancy meeting you here," Slocum said, feeling suddenly a whole lot better about everything.

"I could say the same."

"How are things at the Bathtub Emporium?" he asked.

"I've got a partner now," Ginny said.

"A partner?" And he moved so that she could stand beside him, and as Highpockets approached, he said, "A drink?"

She nodded. "Yeah, I'd like a drink. What I'm saying about a partner is now you can get washed up and have your back scrubbed with two attendants."

"Gee, that sounds pretty good," Slocum said, grinning as they moved to a table on the far side of the room.

Seated, he looked into her eyes. "You've got something on your mind," he said.

"I shouldn't be telling you this, Slocum, but I'm going to."

"First of all, is it all right your talking to me here in Ratigan's whiskey mill?"

"That's part of what I wanted to tell you."

Slocum looked closely at her. Her eyes were strained, and there was a tightness around her jaw which hadn't been there before. "They got to you, of course."

"Yeah."

"How bad was it?"

"Not bad."

"Let me look at you."

She raised her head, and he studied her face. "No marks," he said. "But there are other ways."

"They want me to see you, talk to you, and . . . and all that. And report back."

"It figures that way." Slocum leaned back in his

chair and smiled at her. "You look good."

And all at once a smile broke all over her face. "So do you, Slocum. Boy, so do you!"

Then he was serious. "I told Ratigan that he was to see nobody hurt you. If anything happens, you let me know."

"All right."

She was looking at him, her eyes soft, and her breath more visible to him now as he looked at her throat. She was damn good-looking, he decided. *Damn* good-looking.

"I'm beginning to itch," he said.

"Maybe you need a bath."

"I think so. But what about your partner?"

"I wasn't thinking of including her," Ginny said and scowled ferociously at him.

He laughed. "You don't work here too, do you?"

"No. But I have a friend who does."

"Well, let's go, then."

She was smiling again. "Slocum, I've been dying for you to make love to me."

"Right now let's do a little living for it," he said. But he wasn't looking at her. His eyes were on two men who had come into the Buffalo Bar after he had, and who were seated at a table near the stove in the center of the room.

"Come on," the girl said, starting to get up. And then seeing he was not looking at her, she stopped. "What? What's up?"

"I'll just be a minute." He had risen slowly and now walked over to the pair seated at the table by the cold stove. Their faces were vaguely familiar; he knew they were Ratigan men.

As he approached, one looked up casually. The other had dropped his hands beneath the table and was gazing across the room.

Slocum moved with the speed of a cat. He was in close as he hooked his foot under the chair of the man who had his hands beneath the table; pulling back on the rung, the man lost his balance and Slocum chopped him on the side of his jaw as he went down.

His companion had half drawn his gun when Slocum threw a glass of whiskey in his face and smashed him in the jaw. The first man was struggling to his feet, clawing at his gun, when Slocum flattened him with a kick in the groin, followed by a chopping punch in the back of his neck. As he sank to the floor, Slocum grabbed his gun. He then seized the gun from the second man's holster before he could draw it.

"Get into those chairs," he said, "and listen to this. My friend here and myself are leaving. You are going to stay here. If I even see you or smell you anywhere near me or my friend, I'll tear you apart. Do you understand me?"

"We are under orders not to kill you, Slocum," said the bigger of the pair. "For now," he added grimly.

"I am *not* under orders not to kill you," Slocum said, his words hard and cold as ice. "Just remember that."

He turned and, nodding at Ginny, walked out of the saloon, the girl accompanying him.

When they were out in the street he tossed the two six-guns into a wagon box that was at the hitching post with its team of horses, though first emptying each of ammunition.

"Where can we go?" he asked her.

"I've got a room. Down there." She pointed toward the far side of the tracks, to the area known as the Cabbage Patch. "It isn't going to get us all wet and sudsy, at least." She looked up at him as they went down the street, smiling happily. "But I think you'll like it."

"I expect to," Slocum said. "I expect us both to like it." And he grinned down at her.

"Slocum . . ."

"Uh huh."

"Shiner Ratigan's gonna be awful mad at you when he sees what you done to those gunslingers."

"Are you going to worry about that?"

"No. Not now."

They had crossed the tracks and come to a low, one-story frame shack in the Cabbage Patch, that area reserved for those ladies referred to by the more romantic writers back east as "fallen women."

"It ain't heaven, but it's home," Ginny said as she opened the door

"I'll challenge you on that," Slocum said as he started to undress her. "I do believe I've got some heaven right here in my pants, and I know damn well you've got it in yours."

8

This time she seemed softer; she was softer. He felt her whole body melting into his as they embraced, their arms, their legs around each other, entwined, sealed in a rising passion that each knew would completely dominate them in but a moment.

Their tongues, their hands explored. His penis stroked all around her vagina, while now she gripped it between her hot thighs, riding him, then reaching behind her to tickle its head with her fingers. When he pulled away momentarily, she seized his rigid member and began stroking it. Then she was down on him, taking him deep in her mouth, down her throat, deep down until she gagged and had to come up for air, her face flushed with excitement. He now parted the lips between her legs with his fingers, and sank his longest finger—the middle one—all the way inside, as far as it would go, wiggling it, while she gasped and squirmed, yet made no other sound, thus keeping the intensity within her. Releasing her vagina now he rolled up on top of her, supported on his elbows and knees, preparing to mount her. But she laughed and, slipping down on him, licked his belly button, while her hand grasped his rigid cock, and she guided its head to the soaking lips of her cunt, stroking herself with the head of his great penis, while she laughed softly with sheer ecstasy and wiggled her butt deliciously to tease his organ into still greater rigidity.

And now she slipped further down and took his great thing in her mouth, nearly choking, yet sucking and stroking and licking while with her free hands she played with his balls, the crack of his ass, until Slocum could hardly hold it another moment.

Finally, he mounted her. There was no escaping it this time. Neither could stand even a second's more play. Driving in all the way, he filled her, and soon they settled down to a rhythm which was even and in perfect timing each with each.

Deliriously they rode with the bed screeching and complaining, and it flashed for a split second through Slocum's mind that those wild springs and that beaten-up cornhusk mattress just had to be enjoying it too.

Later, after they had rested and they were lying on their backs close together and holding hands, he said so.

"Gee, Slocum, you know what? I was thinkin' the same thing."

"No fooling?"

"No fooling." She rolled over and kissed him on the cheek. "Know something else?"

"What?"

"I don't see any reason why them springs and that cornhusker shouldn't have some more fun."

"Neither do I," Slocum said, and he rolled over on top of her as her legs fell apart and she encircled him with both arms. Even before he entered her, her buttocks were pumping with delight.

The horse and rider were barely discernible as they came out of the shadow thrown by the big butte. The horse was a blue roan with a dull white blaze on its forehead. He was a chunky piece of horseflesh, durable, and good on the thin, hard mountain trails over which his rider had been traveling.

The man and the horse moved out to the edge of the escarpment that overlooked a big section of the long valley, including a tiny section of the Double R outfit, although a stranger to that country wouldn't have known he was on Double R range.

The rider drew rein and, standing in his stirrups, swept the country about with his field glasses. He was not a big man, but he was wiry and tough and plainly knew horses. He was wearing a Smith & Wesson .45 on his right hip, in a holster that was worn and at the same time looked supple. The gun, as often with this type of range rider, looked as though it had been well used. Its owner looked as though he knew how to use it, young though he was. A man might have guessed him at eighteen, a woman would have said younger.

As his glasses slowly swept the country below

him he spotted the cloud of dust on the far side of the Lazy Water. It could mean only one thing: somebody was running a gather, getting everything in and ready for branding the spring calves. It looked like a big herd coming together. He could discern riders, even one rider who looked to be a roper. But there was another with a loop. Yes, a big herd.

But it was early. They were pulling in their calves early. It reminded him of the time of the war, when the small stockmen had run an early gather to catch the spring calves before the big outfits could get their mitts onto the young stuff. Boy, that had been something. That had been a real excitement.

And now it looked like somebody was pulling the same trick. Yonder, right by the Rocking Box if he was judging it rightly. Yes, the Rocking Box. Lander Miles's place.

Well, it had been a while. And by golly it was funny how he'd just happened to come along at such a time. A time when the action was high and fast. Well, why not? Hell, wasn't that why he was here, to check on the action?

He made another sweep with the glasses, and then slipped them into the battered case. Then he lifted his reins, turned the roan so that he was heading due west, and started along an old game trail that looked as though it hadn't been traveled for a good long while.

The trail wound down through the tall timber, then broke out on a high ledge from which he could see the ranch houses below. He chuckled to himself, realizing that likely no one had ridden that old trail since he had the last time. Nobody much knew about it, in fact.

He reached to the pocket of his shirt then, took out a quirly, and lighted it.

Felix Horne's funeral had finally taken place, an event that had been postponed due to the "accident" that had befallen Lemuel Fang, the coffin maker. And by this time the attention and interest of the citizens of Medicine Butte had almost exhausted itself. Thus, not many attended the ceremony at Boot Hill.

To be sure, Slocum had been there, interested to see what bits and pieces he could pick up about the workings of the town, and especially the situation that was rapidly building to a climax with the Ratigan, or town, faction on the one hand, and the Lander Miles, or cattlemen and range, faction on the other.

The big stockmen had sure enough lost the cattle war in the county, or so it said in the eastern papers, and so some people, even people in high places, thought. But the folks who supported the bars and the cathouses, the barbers and other trade in the towns in Buffalo County had quickly learned otherwise. It was evident now that the "war" between the small stockmen and the big cattle barons had been a skirmish, a battle lost by the big cattlemen and which now had expanded into a major campaign. The big men had the resources. They had the hired gunmen, they had the courts, they had the money and the time and the patience. The small men did not.

But now, surprisingly, out of the blue had come new threats to their hegemony—the railroad, and the land grabbers who were importing immigrants to settle the land, and—at least in Buffalo County—Mr. Ulysses Ratigan, a veritable prince of duplicity, land swindling, influencing, and certainly gunpower.

Slocum realized that the cattlemen, epitomized by Lander Miles, one of their principal leaders, were nonplussed by a man like Shiner Ratigan. Ratigan had no personal ax to grind. He wasn't concerned with his land, his homestead, his cattle, his family, or any of the things that the small stockmen were worried about; he was interested only in power—that is, money, wealth, and influence, of the political variety of course. Ratigan didn't know a cow from a horse, but he could spot gold dust, usable land, and political power with an eye whose speed, accuracy, and cold aggression would have put a baldheaded eagle to shame. Furthermore, Ratigan had nothing to lose. He was risking nothing. He had nothing the cattle barons wanted. They, on the other hand, had plenty that called his greed into play. And the best point, as far as Slocum could see, was that Ratigan had much more freedom of movement than his adversaries. In a certain sense, then, it would appear that Mr. Ratigan had the advantage, insofar as he had less invested in the outcome than the stockmen did. He had nothing to lose.

But then Slocum realized that, on the other hand, the gambler did indeed have a great deal to lose: namely, his high opinion of himself, his reputation throughout the gambling halls of the West, and the great—indeed, for him absolutely necessary—pleasure and need of being on top. A man like Shiner Ratigan only understood winning; he could not entertain the thought, even the possibility, of losing. And so every "game," every effort, no matter how small, was always of the utmost importance.

Therefore, Slocum had become absolutely necessary to his plan, and even more so when Ratigan had learned of the presence of Scarf Sables on the scene. It was clear that Shiner Ratigan always had to have a winner, whether a prizefighter, a cockfighter, a bulldog in the pit, or a gunfighter—his must be the best. Ulysses "Shiner" Ratigan had to be unquestionably the best.

Indeed, it was this summing up of Ratigan that Slocum realized gave him his freedom. For the gambler wouldn't dare risk losing his prize gunslinger. And so Slocum knew right to his bones that in a sense he was more free than any of the Ratigan men. He could almost dictate his own terms. But of course, there was Scarf Sables. Sables was more than likely in a similar position with Lander Miles.

But it couldn't last forever. Sooner or later one side or the other—Ratigan, or Miles and the big cattlemen—would have to make a move.

That morning the wind broke down through the long rock canyons, cut through the tall timber, swept over the rolling green land and across the tawny grass that led to the banks of the Lazy Water, crossed, pushing ripples in its wake, and spent itself in the bunch grass along the breaks on the other side.

High up, though, the wind still pushed against the log cabin, the corral, slamming the gate at one point, the barn, the bunkhouse. But the Double R buildings must have been used to it. In that country, and especially that high up, there was always wind. As Tom Rourke had told it, it was why that country was so good for feed; the wind blowing away the snow kept the stock fat, or at any rate, not too thin. Of course now it wasn't winter and there was no snow to worry about. Still, it was a reminder; the wind, Tom Rourke had always said, was a good reminder.

His eldest daughter, Nellie, remembered this now as the wind tugged at her bandanna, which she had wrapped around her head to keep her hair out of her eyes while she hung the wash. The sheets were flapping big and hard in the wind, slapping her a couple of times across the face and leaving with her the smell of soap. They'll be dry in a minute, she was thinking as she pushed clothespins onto the last one.

All at once she felt the man standing behind her, at the edge of the trees. The feeling just came, it seemed from nowhere, and yet she was sure of it, as indeed she always was sure of her feelings. For a moment she wished it was John Slocum. But she knew that was foolish. A foolish thought. A silly feeling. Yet it was there every now and again, had been ever since he'd spent that time with them and had ridden off one bright morning. It seemed long ago. No, she told herself again, she shouldn't think thoughts like that. Thoughts that led no place. And yet she did.

She didn't turn around to see, though, for there was just a smidgin of hope, and she didn't want the hope to vanish in the glare of reality. Still . . .

But then, she knew it wasn't him, wasn't Slocum. The feeling was different. Where was Caney? Still inside. She hadn't seen or heard her come out. Caney had been in the kitchen. The Henry rifle was in the kitchen too. And it was loaded. And she remembered how Slocum had warned both of them not to go outside alone, but always to have one of them watching, and never to be far away from the Henry. And she remembered now too how kind his face had been when he'd told them this. And again there was the flash of longing, but this was instantly supplanted—by fear? No, not by fear, but by some kind of worry. As though she had forgotten something.

She continued to fold the laundry into her basket, without turning around, without changing the tempo of her movement, as though nothing out of the ordinary was there. And at the same time she felt the presence behind her growing stronger.

"Hello, Nell."

And Nellie Rourke felt something lift and crack all at the same time as she spun around to see Brom standing there at the edge of the trees—in fact, right where their dad had brought down the grizzly that time with the same Henry they'd guarded themselves with all these days and nights. Brom was standing there with his arms at his sides, a little bit swing-hipped like he'd always stood since he started being bigger than a shaver, and with that smile at his lips, like he was about getting ready to tell something real funny.

She didn't hear her own cry break from her as she ran toward him.

He had checked his backtrail carefully and often. And he felt secure that he had shaken Ratigan's men, the pair who had been following him about town and even part of the way along the South Pass Trail until he finally lost them. They were not good trackers, yet Slocum didn't relax his vigilance, even when he was sure they had lost his trail. A man had always to take accident into account. Fools could stumble onto something valuable as easily as wise men. At least, sometimes.

As the dawn began to fill the sky over the high Absarokas he took a careful look through his glasses. He had been following an old game trail up high into the rimrocks, having first ridden over a long sweep of ground stubbled with cactus. Dry, hard, unremitting soil, kin to the volcanic mountain on which it rested.

He sat his spotted pony, sweeping the vista ahead and below, trying to find some landmark that was familiar. And there—yes—there was the Rocking Box, way down and across the river. And so he judged himself to be almost directly over the Double R. Thing was to find a trail down. He knew there had to be another way in to the Rourke place other than coming up right into their horse corral and barn. He had asked Nellie and Caney Rourke about it the last —and only—time he'd been at the Double R. Neither of them knew of another way in, though they had thought there might be, allowing that only their father, and possibly Brom, knew of it.

Slocum was playing a hunch. He hadn't known Tom Rourke, but he knew the caliber of his daughters; he could tell there was something in the family line: good sense. A man like Rourke would insist on having a way out.

The sun was warm on the backs of his hands as he

turned his spotted pony and rode north just behind the lip of the rimrock, so that he was protected from view. He saw the coyote watching him then, and saw him run into a stand of bullberry bushes.

Then he saw the deer tracks. They were no more than two days old. Dismounting, he led the spotted horse into the thick undergrowth, and as his eyes grew accustomed to the darkness inside the timber he began to discern a trail. There were deer prints, and coyote, and at one place he saw the print of a grizzly who had crossed the trail and gone on into the timber toward the west. It was rough going. Here and there a tree had fallen and the trail was blocked. Looking up he kept his bearings by the sun, when he could see it. It was mostly dark within the thick timber, but through the high tops there was always the azure sky, the brightness of the enormous day outside, as the trail led him downward.

In places it was steep and he had trouble with the horse, who now and again spooked at branches whipping back at him, or mostly as the ground gave under his sensitive feet. And then finally they reached a place where the trail widened, at a juncture with a second trail that had also been well traveled by game.

And then he saw the horse tracks. A shod horse, and the tracks fresh, recent, not more than three days old. Seeing the horse balls spread out, he knew the horse was ridden.

Following these tracks, he came to a clearing where evidently the rider had stopped and dismounted. There was a patch of grass that was bent, and obviously he had stood there, probably taking a leak, Slocum figured. Then he had mounted the horse again and crossed the clearing.

He was thinking quickly as he followed the sign. It could mean that whoever it was had already reached the Double R, if that was indeed where he was heading. But who? One of Miles's riders? He didn't think so. Miles wouldn't send his men out alone. They would work in pairs, at the least.

What about Ratigan? Well, the same could be said for the gambler. He was also a man to play an action the sure way. He would not have sent someone alone.

Slocum was reasonably sure that it wasn't somebody who had simply stumbled on the trail by accident. He was certain it was someone who knew where he was, knew where he was heading. Not anybody lost. And at the same time, he noticed with a sudden excitement, someone who had been careless enough to not strip his quirly but who had simply tossed it aside. Slocum examined the butt carefully. The rider had indeed knocked out the ash so that no fire was possible. He'd had that much sense. But he had not destroyed the remaining barrel of the smoke.

Funny, he thought, looking down at the remains of the quirly in the palm of his hand. Funny how a man could be all that careful—as he had seen again and again the rider had been—until that one thoughtless moment when he had tossed the quirly away. •

Trying to form a picture of the rider ahead of him —by maybe a couple of days, he judged it—Slocum continued along the trail, trying to move quickly and carefully at the same time.

He had realized now that the rider might be heading for the Double R. And the hard thought suddenly stood in his mind: Could it be a drygulcher? Was it a hired gun who was maybe even now sighting on his helpless target?

At this point Slocum decided not to spend any more time looking for further sign but to head as quickly as he could for the Double R. There was of course an outside chance that the man ahead wasn't aiming for the Rourke place, though what else he could have been doing there on that nearly inaccessible trail Slocum had no notion.

Shortly he began to see daylight ahead as the trail got even steeper and more difficult for his horse. And then he heard a pistol shot.

It was followed by two more shots, probably from the same gun, and then there was silence.

Even so, highly trained as he had been through his years of tracking, hunting, fighting animal and man, Slocum did not make the mistake of hurrying. As always, he moved quickly but without the slightest hurry. Running Cloud had taught him that years ago —not to move fast or quick, but to *be* quick.

Across the valley, on the other side of the Lazy Water, Lander Miles stood, deep in his tooled riding boots, his California pants, and his stubble of beard, facing his foreman and half a dozen of his men. All were heavily armed, with sidearms and rifles, and most showed bowie knives at their waists. They were hard men, copies of their employer, it could be put, but still not too close to the original. As the saying went, they didn't make men like Lander Miles anymore. Still, these were men he could count on. And they could count on him, too. Count on him to whip them to the ground if they did it wrong, or even thought of arguing something. In the Lazy Water country it was said that Lander Miles was all whang leather and coyote piss. Not a man to get on the wrong side of, for sure.

He was giving instructions. And it was known all through that country that Lander Miles never gave instructions more than once. If you didn't get it the first time, you didn't get it, and you'd best stow your gear and hit the trail.

"We'll move the herd across the river," he was saying, speaking slow and loud. "Ford it at Crazy Man Crossing, then head due north up past the Twin Buttes and then up east to where it's open just before Box Gulch. We'll bed 'em there. There's plenty of room, and the feed is passable."

It was permitted to ask a question, and one cow-poke held up his hand. "That there is close to the Rourke outfit, ain't it?"

"That is so." Lander Miles spat vigorously at a small lizard who managed to get about half of him-self out of the way.

"Lander, what the men want to know is what if somebody from the Rourke outfit don't exactly wel-come us being that close, maybe even on their range?" This question was brought by Chuck-Charlie Snow, the ranch foreman.

Lander Miles looked like he'd swallowed a whole lemon and added a vinegar chaser. "Then they can say so," he said.

"And we'll just hold 'em there, that it?" Chuck-Charlie asked.

"Until I give you a sign otherwise," Lander Miles said, and he looked past his foreman as the door of the main house opened and Scarf Sables came out.

The tall man in black stopped, stood right where he was, with his thumbs hooked into his belt, and said nothing.

"Mount up, then," Miles said, and he took out the makings and began building himself a smoke. He struck a lucifer on the seat of his pants, and lit his cigarette.

When Chuck-Charlie rode up on a strawberry roan horse, as the men were moving toward the herd of cattle, Miles said, "I'll be right along. Want you to just hold 'em. But then when I give you the signal, you and them other six we picked out know what to do."

"Gotcha."

"But you don't do anything without me tellin' it. No matter what happens."

"So we just hold 'em. There ain't much feed up there, Lander. There'll be hardly any after a day or two. What'll they do when they run out?"

"That's what we'll find out, and maybe those Rourkes'll find out."

Chuck-Charlie Snow, knowing very well what would happen, muttered something under his breath, but not anything his boss could notice, as he rode off to his men, who were getting the herd up onto their feet.

A long moment passed while Miles stood there

watching them, smoking his cigarette, and fully aware of Scarf Sables standing nearby.

"Those girls have been given every chance to sell —and at a good price," Miles said. "A goddamn good, fair price. Shit take it!"

"And Slocum?" Sables' voice came softly into the morning air as he stripped off one of his gloves and looked down at a hangnail on his little finger.

"We'll see if this might flush him."

"How long you figure to try holding that herd at Box Gulch, Miles? You think maybe you're pushing a little too fast?"

Lander Miles looked up then, his eyes on an eagle sweeping northward. "By jingo, Sables, I thought you was a man who went for the action, and not the dillydallyin'."

"Action, yes, but does it make sense to push so fast? But it's your business." And he started to turn away.

"It'll be simple," Miles said then. "They'll hold 'em till they get real feisty, see. Maybe let a few head stray onto Double R range, see. We'll show them what could happen, what might happen. You got it? Then we pull back and give them one more chancet to sell."

"And if they don't sell, you'll run 'em through."

"Right through that whole goddamn place. Nothin' like a big-size stampede to straighten things out, now is there?"

"I agree with you there, but what I'm thinking of—and I'm not so sure you are—is Slocum."

"I am thinking of Slocum," Miles said, hard. "That's where you come in. You want backup men?"

"What I am saying," Sables said patiently, "is that right then and there might not be the moment for Slocum to leave this world. It has to be done right. I'm going to call him out, not drygulch him."

"I know that. I know that, God damn it, Sables! But I want you to take care of Slocum, before . . . before the herd is stampeded. Hell, man, maybe we won't even have to stampede those beeves. You think any sensible cattleman wants to run beef off his herd just like that?"

Scarf Sables suddenly let fly a long, thin stream of saliva. It wasn't quite in the direction of the cattleman, but it could have been taken that way; and it could have been intended that way.

Scarf Sables' black eyes were hard as marbles as he watched the rancher tighten into a rock.

"And Miles," he said, his words soft with whisper, patience, and extra meaning, "do you think even for a second that any sensible gunfighter is going to let you or Slocum decide when the action will take place?"

9

"Well, it looks like I come back at just the right time," the young man with the long hands and quick eyes was saying.

"Oh Brom, I can't believe you're really here!" Nellie was staring at him, drinking him in with her large eyes.

Every now and again Caney would reach out to touch him. "Why didn't you write us!" she said again.

"I told you, Caney. I was afraid the law was after me. Didn't want them to track me down through a letter."

He had a soft voice and a quiet smile. They had been talking together all that afternoon and late into the night, trying to catch up, trying to make up for the lost time since he had ridden away on that grim day of the killing.

"It's forgotten now," Nellie said. "At least by the town. Maybe the big ranchers are still holding it against you—if they ever did—I don't know. But so many people have told us over this past time that you were right. That you did the right thing."

"But you're going to stay now, aren't you, Brom?" Caney insisted.

"Looks like I might be needed."

"Brom . . ." Nellie touched his knee with her fingertips. "We don't want any killing, do we?"

"We don't want our place taken away from us, Nellie. Like I said, I came home at the right time."

"There's Mr. Slocum," Caney said. And she told him all about the adventure with the man she had shot at.

"Where's this man at? Why ain't he out here helping you two, if he's so all-fired great?" Brom demanded, his face hardening.

"Brom, he *has* been helping us. I've heard how he's been asking questions in town, and trying to find out things. And I know he'll come see us when he can, and he'll help us."

Brom Rourke was suddenly looking at his sister in a funny way. "You sweet on him, huh, Nell?"

Nellie's cheeks turned almost crimson in that same second, and Caney started to giggle.

But the moment of embarrassment passed, and then they were talking about family things, things that had happened when they'd all been together— before the cattle trouble, when they'd been children together.

And then it was time to go to bed, but they stayed

up talking until it was late. Finally, it really was enough.

As they were saying good night and Caney had stepped away into the kitchen, Nellie said, "You'll stay. You'll stay, won't you, Brom?"

"Yep. I'll stay."

"And . . . are you in any trouble?" She asked this softly, gently, as was her way, and looked down at her hands.

"No, Sis. No, I'm not in any trouble."

In the morning Brom told them that somebody was watching the place. He had risen early and had saddled up and scouted the surrounding country. When he returned the sun was just coming up. "There's someone down below the icehouse, two men. I didn't get up close. I don't know who they are."

He confronted them with this information as Nellie was pouring him a cup of coffee and Caney was putting baking powder biscuits in the oven.

Nellie put down the coffeepot. "Oh, Brom. Do you suppose they're some of Lander Miles's men?"

"I don't know, sis." His eyes swept the room. "You got any other guns besides that Henry?"

"That's it, except for Dad's old Colt in the chest of drawers there."

She'd hardly spoken when there was a knock at the door and Brom Rourke was on his feet with his gun in his fist. He signaled the girls to get away from the door. "Ask who it is, Nell."

But before the girl could speak, the voice came

through the door. "Hello in there. It's Slocum. John Slocum."

And then with a squeal Caney ran forward and pulled open the door and threw herself into Slocum's arms.

Slocum was equal to the occasion, giving her a mighty hug, while at the same time his eyes found Nellie and he grinned happily at her.

In a moment the girls were both talking to him. Brom was hanging back, but shortly, with coffee and fresh baking powder biscuits, they were all at home.

"I reckon that was your horse's tracks I followed down from the rimrocks," Slocum said to Brom with a grin. "Pretty sturdy little animal."

Brom grinned back at him. "That he is. You come from town?"

Slocum nodded.

Suddenly they fell silent. The festivity of greeting each other was over, and suddenly the seriousness of the situation they were facing was upon them.

"I'd been meaning to come out sooner," Slocum said, "but I couldn't. Still, I've got some things to tell you."

"About Lander Miles?" Brom asked.

"Some."

Then Nellie told him about the man in black who had come by and offered them a price for their ranch.

"That's got to be Sables."

"Sables?" Brom's eyebrows shot up. "Scarf Sables?"

"That's the one," Slocum said.

"I heard of him," Brom said. "Supposed to be the fastest gun around. At least that's what some say."

"Well, he's working for Lander Miles," Slocum said.

"He said he was an associate of Mr. Miles," Nellie said. "I didn't like him. He . . . he frightened me."

"What's he doing with Miles?" Brom wanted to know.

"Miles has a lot of gunmen," Slocum said, "from what I've been able to pick up. Also, you should know that there is a herd of cattle over at a place called Box Gulch, near here. You likely know the place. I spotted them coming down just now."

"Box Gulch is right on the line of our range," Caney said. "What are they doing there?"

"I think it's Box Gulch—the name," Slocum said. "Just northeast of here." He pointed with his whole hand, holding his fingers together like he was slicing a line through the air.

"That's the direction," Brom said. "Were they moving 'em in any particular direction?"

"No. They were just being held there."

"Funny."

"Why would they hold a herd of cattle at Box Gulch?" Nellie asked. "That's real poor feed over there."

"Could be they want you to know they're there," Slocum pointed out. "Kind of like trying to push a little."

"They try coming through here to get up onto Elbow for their summer feed, they're going to be in trouble," Brom said.

Slocum nodded at him. "I see you got a good head on your shoulders. That's the only reason for it, far as I can see. They're warning you that that's what can happen or likely will happen unless you sell."

"But they can't do that!" Caney said. "That's against the law. It's our range here!"

"The law," Brom said slowly, "is this." And quick as a wink he had his six-gun in his hand.

Slocum had to admire his speed. "Was that you I heard shooting yesterday?" he said.

Brom nodded.

"Target practice. That's what it sounded like," Slocum said.

The boy grinned. "I see you know guns, mister."

"It don't hurt to know everything," Slocum said. And then he added, "In this country."

"But what are we going to do?" Caney asked. "We can't just do nothing. Nellie, Brom, think of something."

"The first thing is not to get so excited," Nellie said gently and patted her sister on the knee.

Slocum leaned forward in his chair. "The first thing is to have some more of those delicious biscuits, Caney." And he grinned at her.

Blushing furiously, she rose and went to the stove.

When she returned with a loaded plate, Slocum said, "Did anyone else approach you about the Double R?"

"Oh, I almost forgot." Nellie's mouth formed an "O" of shock as she suddenly remembered her encounter in town with Ratigan. "I forgot, a Mr. Ratigan wanted to 'help us,' as he put it. Said he could find a lawyer and all that sort of thing. I forgot about it, because I couldn't figure out what he was really after. Though I think he himself wanted the ranch."

"Has he been around since?" Slocum asked.

Nellie shook her head. "That was in town that I ran into him, or rather he sought me out. No, I haven't heard anything from him since. Oh, and he did definitely say that Lander Miles wanted our place, and that's mainly why he was offering to help."

"So they both want it," Brom said. "Excepting I dunno this feller Ratigan."

"He owns a saloon in town," Slocum said. "And near as I can figure out, he runs the town, owns a lot of it, and wants more. He wants this place." He paused and took a drink of coffee. "The question is why. Why would a man like Ratigan want the Double R? I can see why Miles would want it—as a route for his herd to get onto the mountain for summer feed. But Ratigan? I dunno."

"And why does Miles need to come through here to get up on Elbow Mountain?" Brom asked. "What's wrong with the route those ranches across the river always used to take?"

"I heard there's been a landslide someplace. Blocked the old trail," Slocum said, "leaving this as the only way."

Nellie and Caney Rourke both nodded at that. And Slocum suddenly remembered Shiner Ratigan trying to hire him that first time, saying how he had some deal going about getting cattle up onto the mountains for summer feed. Strange how he'd all but forgotten that particular point. Had Ratigan been working with Miles at that point, or had he simply been trying to confuse him? Had he been trying to get him to think Ratigan was bigger than he actually was? Or was Ratigan thinking ahead to taking over

Miles Lander's place? And suddenly it hit him. Maybe Shiner Ratigan was after the Rocking Box, and not the Double R at all. Maybe that was just a feint, to draw attention away from his grab for the Rocking Box. And then, if so, why would the gambler want the Rocking Box?

Slocum stood up.

"You off somewhere?" Caney said suspiciously, a frown on her young face.

He laughed. And then made a mock frown at her. "I'm heading into town. You ladies have Brom to look after you. You don't need me."

"Yes we do!" they both said almost in unison. And Slocum and Brom both laughed at the way they immediately tried to cover up.

"I've got some checking to do," he said. "And then I'll be back. Meanwhile, keep a close watch. A very close watch. Maybe you'd better even sleep in shifts."

He realized then that it was only now hitting the girls. Until now there had been the fun and the happiness of being together, even though there was the danger, but now with him leaving, the danger was closing in.

Yet he saw no other way. He had to go.

It had been Slocum's intention after he checked in at the Shirley Hotel to contact Lemuel Fang. He knew that the carpenter had completely recovered from his shooting encounter and was back at work, yet Slocum hadn't seen him since his own release from prison.

Still wary of being tracked by Ratigan's gunmen,

he had taken special pains on leaving the Double R to elude any encounters or even to leave a trail that any of the Ratigan men would pick up. So far he had managed successfully, and today was no exception. No one had cut his trail, and he reached Medicine Bluff without any confrontations.

He found Lem Fang building a cabinet in his shop for a customer who had had it on order for nearly a year.

"Just never did get around to it," the old man explained to Slocum, apparently for no good reason at all.

"Can you tell me why those men shot you, Lem?" Slocum asked after they had settled down a bit and were chatting while Fang went about his business.

"Can't say." Lem kept right on with his work, not giving anything to his visitor except the back of his head and now and again some innocuous observation.

"Got a notion who they were?"

"Nope."

"Ratigan men, do you reckon?"

"Dunno."

"Well, that's your business. But you know, I got hauled into jail on account of that shooting, and that's why I'm trying to find out who did it. Thought you could help me."

Lemuel Fang said nothing.

"Want a drink?" Slocum asked. He'd brought along a bottle of Old Overholt just in case.

"If you think you're gonna get me drunk and talkin', you're makin' a bigger mistake than Custer did at the Little Bighorn."

"Well, let's hope I don't end up like that poor gentleman."

A kind of a smile creased the old man's face at that. He put down his tools and accepted the bottle and took a generous slug. "Sure puts lead in the right place, don't it?"

Slocum nodded. "Sure does." He found himself looking at a knapsack and a shovel and pick leaning against a wall of the room. "You ever do any prospecting, Lem?" he asked casually.

"Not much to dig for in this part of the country," Lemuel said, taking another slug of the whiskey. "Did some panning up around Alder Gulch, but I never hit it rich."

"I spotted a burro outside the Buffalo Bar on my way in, and it was pretty well loaded down with digging tools. Funny thing, that. Wouldn't you say?"

"What the hell, maybe some feller hit it. Why not?"

"I never heard of there being anything to dig for in this country," Slocum said.

"There wasn't anything at the Gulch till some jasper found it. What the hell."

The liquor was definitely working, and Slocum was feeling the old man loosening up. "That's a strong pick you got there," he said after another long moment of silence.

A chuckle rolled out of Lem's throat now. "Slocum, by God, you got more questions than a dog's got fleas."

"Only way to find out something is by God to ask," Slocum replied smoothly. "I'm a stranger in this town, and I damn near got stretched for shooting you, which I didn't do, and you wonder why I'm asking questions."

"Well, hell, I just got that stuff there like I got a lot of things around my shop here."

"It wasn't here last time I was in," Slocum said, pressing.

"Well, for the matter of that, I didn't have an itch on the end of my ass last time you was in neither. So what does that mean?" And he reached again for the bottle.

And then, all at once, out of nowhere as it were, Lem Fang said, "You'll want to watch your step, Slocum. I shouldn't be tellin' you this, but I recollect you was the one tried to help when them jaspers shot at me." He belched suddenly, and looked solemn.

"Know who it was tried to hit you?"

"I got a notion, but I won't say it. Bad luck to talk about things like that." He took another pull at the bottle. "Only thing I can rightly say is it warn't that sonofabitch in his fancy black suit."

The reference to Scarf Sables quickened the excitement in Slocum which had begun with his companion opening up. "How so? How do you know that?"

"On account of that sonofabitch wouldn't have just wounded me. Huh!" He snorted, licking his tongue along his lips. "But I got settled with him. I am free, shut of that, and the bastard knows it."

"You've been talking to him, to Sables?"

"He come in here, tried to frighten me. I wasn't scared." He turned right toward Slocum then. "You want to know something, young feller? I wasn't scared of the sonofabitch. By God, I was really,

really shut of it." A chuckle escaped him suddenly, almost like a sudden cough.

"Shouldn't be tellin' you all this stuff, but I want the whole world to know I'm free, and I feel like a million dollars." Another chuckle broke from him then. "No, not a million dollars. A gold mine. I'm feelin' like I was the richest gold mine in the whole fucking West."

"That must be a good feeling," Slocum said, moving the bottle slightly out of reach of his companion, for it was clear the old man was about to fall asleep or else become incoherent. He'd surely had enough.

Indeed, Lemuel Fang's eyes had closed, and there was a beatific smile on his face as he mumbled, "All those years ascairt of that sonofabitch. He knew I'd rode with the gang. Knew it, like nobody else, on account all the others 'ceptin' him and me was dead." His eyes were closed, but he was still talking, mumbling some, and here and there Slocum had trouble following.

"What gang were you riding with, Lem?" Slocum asked.

The man was almost falling out of his chair now, but he managed to open his eyes. "Gimme drink."

"Who were you riding with?" Slocum asked again.

"Not like that, young feller. It was who was riding with me. I din't ride with nobody. They rode with me! Until that sonofabitch come along. Young he was then, but I was still older. A good bit older, and . . . slower. He got me. Got my guts. Then, then . . . the other night. The other . . . was free."

A snore broke from the old man, and Slocum stood up and turned down the coal-oil lamp and walked out of the carpenter shop. He was wondering who old Lemuel Fang had been back in the days when he'd known Scarf Sables. Not that that was so important. The pick and shovel were important, and the loaded burro he'd seen outside the Buffalo Bar.

But when he got down to the Buffalo, the burro was no longer there.

He was walking back to the carpenter shop to see how the old man was when he heard the single pistol shot. He knew exactly where it came from. And he knew that this time the bullet was not for wounding. Old Lem Fang was truly free.

Like any successful man in his profession, Ulysses Ratigan fully understood that the principle behind such old reliables as the coin-in-the-cake game, the shell game, and three-card monte was absolutely basic to any felicitous enterprise. The simpler, the more obvious the bait, the quicker and more surely the mark bit. The underlying motive was always and inevitably avarice. This was the rule. It always had been and always would be. Everybody knew it, but only the happy few understood it. Ulysses Ratigan prided himself on being one of the rare happy few. And he surely was. For he knew that what worked in the time of the caveman worked anytime, anyplace, and with anybody.

"My dear, that was delightful," Shiner was saying as he rose from the bed after disentangling himself from his companion of the night.

"Bunny, I'm going to miss you." Vera's sleepy

voice came from the bedclothes, while her hand reached out and stroked his buttock as he sat on the edge of the bed.

"My dear, I would love to dally further," Shiner whispered, "but today is a big day, and I must face my fate. Perhaps this evening we can lock horns again."

There was no arguing the point, Vera realized, and pouting just a little—not enough to annoy him, for she knew very well how to play him, and knew too how not to step over the line—pouting attractively, and with a cute wiggle of her bare bottom, she too began to get dressed.

By the time Shiner was downstairs he had forgotten her. The barroom was deserted save for Highpockets Purdy, who was rubbing the top of the mahogany bar, and Jules, the old swamper, who was pushing a broom over the floor and would presently spread fresh sawdust.

"Coffee?" Highpockets asked as he swiftly and expertly studied his employer's mood.

Shiner Ratigan nodded. "And a steak and eggs and spuds. Some biscuits, too. Lots of coffee. If you don't have the grub go across to the On Time and get it."

Highpockets nodded, and poured from the pot he kept at the end of the bar. "An eye-opener?"

Shiner pursed his lips, as though turning this over. "You talked me into it, my lad."

Highpockets grinned and reached for the bottle.

"I saw that interesting pack animal at the hitch rail last night," Shiner said as he lifted his glass. And he cocked his head at Highpockets, nodded a little toward the old swamper to make sure he was within earshot, and said, "Don't tell me Medicine Butte's up for a gold strike."

"By God, you reckon it?" Highpockets picked up perfectly on Shiner's lead. "Mr. Ratigan, I heard there wasn't any gold around these parts since Christ was a corporal. I mean, one old prospector don't make a bonanza."

"Oh, I don't think there's anything, Highpockets," Shiner replied calmly, playing with his glass of morning brandy. "I don't really reckon so. By the way, where the hell is my breakfast?"

"Coming, coming. I sent Jake for it."

And at that exact moment Jake walked in from the back of the saloon with Shiner Ratigan's breakfast.

He was a man who had very few teeth, but these he was sucking vigorously in his excitement, almost spilling the steak and eggs as he delivered his news from the On Time Cafe.

"Millie at the On Time says she's heard there was gold somebody brought in. Found it up around the North Fork." His face was aglow as with shaking hands he placed the platter before Shiner Ratigan.

At that point, Jules, the swamper, put down his bucket of sawdust, leaned his broom against the corner of the room, and departed swiftly through the swinging doors.

Shiner caught the movement. "Looks like there's gold in them thar hills," he announced with a big grin, and picking up his knife and fork began to savage his steak.

As he was chewing happily on his first cut, the

batwing doors flew open and three men entered. "Boss, you heard what happened?"

"What?" Shiner Ratigan's face was a study in innocence.

"Gold. Gold up by the North Fork."

"You figure it's true, boss?" asked another of the trio. "Could be just gossip."

"Interesting," said Shiner as he cut thoughtfully into his steak. "Interesting how both of those words —gold and gossip—start with a 'g.'" And he winked at Highpockets. "Anybody see that old prospector who was in here last night?"

"Somebody said he was down in the livery."

"Go take a look, one of you. I want to talk with him," Shiner said, all business now. "You others, check around town. See what you can find out. But don't go spreading it around about gold. We don't want folks getting all excited about a false alarm. You know, it could be some bunco feller, maybe even that old prospector, selling the old snake oil to this town." And he winked broadly at the men who had gathered around him.

In a few moments the saloon began to fill, and the air was thick with questions.

Shiner Ratigan was still trying to finish his breakfast, supported by a second brandy and surrounded by a number of his own men, whom he had previously told to appear.

By now the saloon was almost filled, with everyone talking at once about the possibility of a gold strike. Yet no one seemed to be sure where.

Into this hive of eager auguring on the possibilities of wealth now came the man who had gone looking for the old prospector, who evidently had spent the night in the livery.

"He's gone. His burro's gone. There ain't hide nor hair of him. Eli said he only slept about an hour, then pulled out. Real early. On account of he was gone when Eli come in this morning."

"Did he pay Eli for his board?" someone with a practical mind asked.

"Jesus!" someone muttered with disgust. "At a time like this, Sam, you're worried over a man paying for his overnight when there could be thousands, millions out there wherever the hell he's headin'."

"I says we send someone after that old jasper," someone said at the back of the crowd. "Find out for sure what's going the hell on."

At this point Shiner Ratigan rose from his table, belched softly, and held up his hands for quiet.

That took a moment, with lots of hushing and swearing, and at one point even a shove, but the room quieted.

"Men, I don't know what's going on," Shiner said. "But we'll find out. Just don't get yourselves all riled up. I don't believe there's gold anywhere around Medicine Butte. Why, I looked into that when I first came out here. The country ain't right for it. The rock formations and like that, at least around this part. Up around the North Fork, well, I dunno. But don't start gettin' everybody all jangled up. Let's keep it quiet till we're sure."

"Time we are sure everybody else in town'll have staked hisself a prime section," someone shouted from the back of the crowd.

Suddenly there was a yell from the other side of the room and a fight started.

"It's Harold," somebody said. "He found somethin' when he went down to the livery lookin' for the prospector."

"Quiet! Quiet!" Shiner Ratigan bellowed the words as he stood on a table. "Now you men come to your senses! Harold, what you got there?"

"Nothing. I was just going out. I ain't et yet and I'm hungry."

Someone shouted, "What the hell's all this fussin' about? That prospector feller was in here last night. Didn't anybody talk to him, see what he was up to?"

"Now we got some sense comin' in at last," Shiner said. "Look, you men, that prospector was in here and had one drink—just one. You can ask Highpockets here. I saw him. And then he left. Nothing in that. It happens all the time. So what the hell is everybody getting so all-fired hot about?"

"He's probably sleeping out on the trail someplace," a voice at the back of the room called out.

"Absolutely." Shiner Ratigan said the word with the finality that should have finished the whole discussion.

Only now someone else called out from the crowd, "Maybe that old boy *is* sleeping out on the trail someplace, but ten'll get you twenty he's goosing his ass all the way to wherever that gold is."

"There ain't no gold!"

"Then take a look at what Harold found in the livery where the old bastard got some feed for his burro."

The voice was quiet, and magically the room quieted instantly.

"What you got there, Harold?" Shiner asked quietly, but loud enough for all to hear.

"Just this," Harold said, and he held up the object that he had found in the livery.

In the incredible silence that followed, Shiner Ratigan moved through the crowd to face Harold Winterhagen, a half-breed who had been in his employ a number of years; a man, moreover, who was an excellent shot, and knew very well what he was holding in his hand.

Shiner Ratigan took the object from him and examined it. "You say you found this in the livery?"

Harold Winterhagen nodded. "Yup. Right near the tack room, where that man was standing when he went to get feed for his animal."

"How do you know he was standing there?"

"Willie told me, the hostler's boy. He was there when I went down to see if I could find him, the old man, and Willie showed me this. He let me have it, on account of I said I had to show it to you."

"Then why didn't you show it when I asked what you had there before?"

"Dunno."

The room was still as a cemetery as the men crowded to get a look at the nugget.

In a few moments, however, the group began to stir out of their shock, and a thrill ran through the room.

Shiner had been waiting for the moment, and now he dealt his ace. "Number one, I ain't so sure that's real gold," he said solemnly. "And number two, I ain't so sure some bunco artist isn't trying to slicker us."

Being a professional he had no trouble in suppressing the grin that was racing through him as he saw how the crowd was swallowing it.

And he said it again. "I think somebody's trying to slicker this town. I'm going to have this investigated." His words fell into the barroom solemn as a judge's. "Someone is trying to run a scam here. Well, by God they ain't gonna get away with it. I'm going to have this rock assayed. Meanwhile it'll stay in my safe. Highpockets . . ."

"Yeah, boss?"

"You hold on to this till I come back. Then we'll lock it up." He paused. "And Harold, you stay with him." He raised his voice for the crowd jamming the room. "You men cool down now. I've seen this kind of thing before. We don't want to make damn fools of ourselves."

And with a nod at nobody in particular he pushed his way through the crowd, which did its best to open for him.

Outside three men were waiting for him. They were mounted and they held an extra horse.

"We'll ride out slow," Shiner said. "I want to be sure everyone sees me leaving town. And from under the brim of his hat his eyes swept the crowd that was now rapidly forming in the street. And when he heard the words "Up to the North Fork, up by the Rourke place," this time he didn't restrain his smile.

10

Slocum heard it almost the moment it hit the street. He'd heard it before, in other towns, and he knew well the special ring the word "gold" carried. He had seen what it did to men. He'd been in a couple of gold strikes; he knew the feel, the taste, the smell of it. And he knew too that it was beside the point whether or not the strike was true or false. The point was that the attention of the entire town and the neighboring country was now turned toward the North Fork of the Lazy Water River. Toward the country surrounding the Rourke Double R—and also, with the possibility of including it.

When he got down to the livery he got the story about the gold nugget, and by then he was pretty sure the whole thing was a con. He saddled and bridled his pony carefully, but not wasting any time.

"How long ago did that fellow come looking for

169

the prospector?" he asked Billy, the boy in charge at that hour of the morning.

"That breed feller?"

"I dunno. Somebody heard about the prospector and then came looking for him, at least that's what I was told."

"Early. And he found a nugget there where the old man had been checking his burro."

"Jesus," muttered Slocum. "People will believe anything."

"Huh?" Billy said. He was not a very bright boy, and his mouth hung open and he drooled a little.

"Nothing." And he handed money to the youth. "One other thing. Did you see where Mr. Ratigan went? Which way?" Slocum was taking a chance that Ratigan had in fact left town, and that the boy could have seen him.

"Headed thataway," Billy said, jerking his thumb toward the trail leading north out of town.

"Two men with him, were there?"

"Three," Billy said. And Slocum handed him another silver dollar.

When he rode out into the street he saw the crowd gathered and heard the shouting; and, turning to the boy, Billy, he said, "You're going to have a run on horseflesh, my lad. Better brace yourself for it."

Billy grinned.

"You said Ratigan and his men were heading east, did you?"

"North," the boy said, coming close so he didn't have to speak loudly. "North, Mr. Slocum."

• • •

North, Mr. Slocum. As he rode away he heard those words the boy had said once again and realized that, yes, maybe there were some people in Medicine Butte who didn't buy Shiner Ratigan and his gang all the way. Maybe.

He rode quickly but not pushing, watching for sign and making sure nobody was following him. It was clear now that Ratigan also wanted the Double R. But why? Or was it that he was really against Lander Miles having it. Was he simply trying to foil Miles? Or did he want Miles's Rocking Box?

And what about Miles? He wanted and needed a way up to the mountain. And the only way, with the old way under a landslide, was right through the center of the Rourke spread. There was simply no other solution except going extra miles around by Charlie's Crossing.

Well, that was clear, clean, and simple, Slocum reasoned. That was the way any cattleman would look at the situation. Plus the fact that Miles would of course reckon the Double R was rightfully his since he'd staked his former hand Rourke to settle there.

And so the stockman was trying to push, and if necessary he'd soon shove, and then if that wasn't enough to make the Rourkes give in, he'd run his cattle right through their place. It was hell on a herd to stampede it, it'd run a lot of pounds off them, but it was better than having them starve to death. And of course it'd be out of the question for the Rourke girls to agree to let the herd through in the first place. The only route was right through where their ranch houses stood.

But Miles would hear of the gold rumor, which even by now could have built up into a true gold rush, with everybody in the country closing in on the North Fork with pick and shovel and panniers and burros and guns and booze and all the damn rest of it. Slocum had seen what gold did to people. And yet, it wasn't really gold that did it so much as it was the thought of gold. The dream of it. The greed for it.

Only wait a minute, stay with the cattle drive, he told himself. There was a way around the landslide. Miles could push his herd across the river at Charlie's Crossing. It would take another day, according to the map he'd looked at. No, the point to see was that it wasn't the route to Elbow Mountain that Miles wanted so much as it was the Rourke spread itself. That became clear now as he thought it through again. Obviously, Miles was eager to consolidate the whole of the northern range above Medicine Butte—Miles and the men behind him too, the stockgrowers. Evidently there was a plan for even more land grabbing, and the Rourke place was only one step on the way, yet a wholly necessary one. Otherwise, why hire someone like Sables? Those big stockgrowers didn't spend money unnecessarily.

Sables. The pieces began to fit now. On the surface it might not seem so obvious to the people in Medicine Butte, or to anyone else either, but the Buffalo County war was definitely not over. Slocum knew that his next move had to be at the Rocking Box, but first he had to warn the Rourkes of the likelihood of visitors looking for gold.

•   •   •

At Box Gulch the Rocking Box herd was restive. They had reached the benchland near the Lazy Water a good eighteen hours before, and Miles's men were holding the beeves there. It wasn't easy, though, as the feed had gotten cropped and the cattle needed to move. But it was what Lander Miles had ordered, and that was reason enough.

Miles himself had only just arrived, riding up on a neat little chestnut pony with a wide white blaze on his forehead and four white stockings, and he was followed by Sables within another hour.

The owner of the Rocking Box brand stood now in the early forenoon under a lowering sky, listening to the bawling of the herd, a tin cup of coffee in one hand and a chunk of sourdough bread in the other.

"Fixin' to storm," Chuck-Charlie Snow observed, clomping up on his high-heeled boots, letting his words reach Miles across a saddle rig that was lying on the ground near the chuck wagon.

"Might." Miles squinted at the low sky, canting his head. Then he scratched his nose, sniffed, and took another sip of coffee. He looked over at Scarf Sables, who was drinking coffee over by the wagon, but said nothing.

"Rider comin' in," Chuck-Charlie said.

"I heard him." Miles had just emptied his cup and dumped the grounds onto a clump of sage when one of his outriders came in.

"It's that feller Slocum coming," he said, drawing rein.

"Alone?"

"Alone."

Miles looked over to where Sables had been

standing with his coffee, but the man in black was no longer there.

In the next moment John Slocum came riding into the circle of men and drew rein.

Lander Miles squinted up at the man on horseback. "What do you want, Slocum?"

"I've come to tell you you'll never make it through the Double R. Shiner Ratigan's started a gold-rush panic, and by the time you get there you'll find more men with shovels and guns than you can handle. I mean the whole town, plus they'll be there digging gold. They won't exactly be welcoming you and your beeves."

The boss of the Rocking Box brand looked like he'd been whipped in the face. "Gold! What the hell you sayin' there? There ain't no gold within a thousand miles of here. You've gone plumb loco."

"The town has gone plumb loco, Miles, not me. If you don't believe me, send a couple of riders over to have a look."

Lander Miles continued to stand there, squinting up at the man on horseback, still not believing it.

"You don't believe me, Miles, but go take a look."

"Charlie." Miles still kept his eyes on Slocum, reading him for the straight of it. "Send a couple riders. Meanwhile, Slocum here can wait with us."

"I don't think so, Miles. I've got work to do."

"My men there have got you covered."

"You'd shoot me down just like that? I didn't know that was your style, Miles. Somebody's been teaching you bad habits."

Lander Miles dropped his eyes away from Slocum

now as he watched two men peel away from his cadre, under instructions from Chuck-Charlie Snow, and head for the Double R.

"Good enough, Slocum. I got no fight with you."

"Miles, don't you think you ought to send some more men and guns over to the Rourke place to see what Ratigan's up to?"

"I don't trust you, Slocum."

"Then why'd you send those riders? Does that mean you trust Ratigan?"

"It means I want to move my beeves up onto Elbow Mountain, and I aim to move 'em through the Rourke place."

"You don't have to go that way."

"There ain't no other way."

"You can push through Charlie's Crossing."

"That's way the hell an' gone out of my way."

"It'd take you an extra day. Not all that bad."

"Listen, that outfit yonder, that place yonder is rightly part of this here, and I aim to have it. Rourke cheated me, and I'm gonna get that range back."

"Miles, that's all past history. Bury it. Those girls own that place now, and no court of law is going to say otherwise. You know that. I know it."

"I don't know it."

Slocum had heard the man approaching, but had not turned to see who it was. He knew, however. And now, still without looking, he dismounted, with his horse standing between himself and Scarf Sables.

"Maybe you and Sables can settle that," Miles said.

"You get other men to do your fighting for you, Miles? Hell, I thought you was one of them tough old cattlemen who fought the Indians and built the West and all that." Slocum had stepped away from his horse now, and had slapped him on the rump so that he'd get out of the way.

"Don't rile me, Slocum."

"You got Sables to do your fighting for you?"

"Let me take him," Sables said, cutting in. "Miles, I'll take the sonofabitch."

"In the back, like you did Lem Fang, huh, Sables?" Slocum knew he had to stall, he had to play for time and mostly position. "I'm surprised at you, Miles," he said. "But then, I suppose you big stock-growers don't mind a little murder now and again, like you did Tom Rourke."

As he talked, and caught their attention, little by little he was moving into a fresh position.

"You boys going to cross-fire me, Miles? Or am I going to get you each at a time?"

Miles was red in the face, chewing on his lower lip as Slocum's hot words burned into him. He was a proud man, but damnit, it wasn't right two girls using the fact that they was women to take advantage like they'd been doing. No, by God, it wasn't right.

"I'll take him, Miles," Scarf Sables said again.

"Will you?" said Slocum. "Then why don't you tell Miles to drop his gun? Tell him to unbuckle."

And then another voice suddenly cut into the circle of men, all of whom were caught up in the drama of Slocum and his two adversaries.

"I've got 'em covered, Slocum. I've got whichever one covered you want." And Brom Rourke stepped into view.

But before Slocum could speak, two men who had

been behind the chuck wagon sprang out and wrestled the boy to the ground.

In the next instant Scarf Sables struck for his gun.

Slocum was loose in every part of his body, loose and at the same time with the right balance of tension where it was needed. To the men watching it was as though his gun leapt from its holster into his hand and he had drilled the man in black right through the heart.

Scarf Sables, his face torn in surprise, dropped to the ground. And Slocum instantly had Lander Miles covered. But the cattleman had not gone for his gun. His hands had dropped to his sides, and they stayed there.

Neatly, Slocum holstered his .45 and stood looking down at the dead gunman who always wore black.

"Why the hell did he always wear black?" Lander Miles suddenly asked, speaking to no one in particular.

"Who knows?" Slocum said. "Maybe the color matched his insides." He turned to Miles. "Me and Brom will be riding out now. I do believe our business is settled."

He walked over to his spotted horse and mounted up. "Miles, I look at it like you made a mistake. It's done now. Things can start over. You can take your herd over Charlie's Crossing. I'll be around awhile, helping out at the Double R."

Miles had finally recovered from his shock. He ran the palm of his hand across his face, and stared again at the body of Scarf Sables. "Couple you men get him into that box wagon and he can get planted in town," he said grimly quiet.

He turned to Slocum and Brom, who were both mounted now. Being Texas, Lander Miles didn't give up easily. "You were lucky, Slocum."

"I wasn't lucky, Miles. I was better than that punk you hired to do your dirty work for you."

He turned and nodded to Brom Rourke, and they kicked their ponies into a brisk canter.

When they were out of sight of the Miles herd and crew Slocum drew rein.

"I want you to get on back to your outfit," he said. "Were there any people around when you rode over?"

"No one. Where you going?" Brom asked.

"I'm heading for town. Now, anybody comes there, you tell them you saw me, and that Sables is dead, and Miles is moving his cattle back to his range."

"Sure. But why don't you come over. We'll need all the help we can get."

"Young feller," Slocum said, and his tone was really kind, "you had better do a whole lot better than you did with those Rocking Box cowboys if you want to get to be twenty-one."

Brom Rourke flushed right up into his hat. "I *am* twenty-one," he said. "And I know they caught me off guard, but next time—"

"Young man," Slocum said, "I'm going to give you one piece of advice. Just one. And don't you forget it. There is never any 'next time.' Just remember that. There is only this time. Every time is this time. And another thing, I told you to stay there with your sisters when I was over there just a while back."

Then, with a brief nod, he laid his reins across his pony's neck and kicked him into the trail toward Medicine Butte.

He rode quickly toward town, though without pushing his horse. He didn't want him tired out when he got there. It was always a bad notion to arrive anywhere on an exhausted mount.

When he reached Medicine Butte it was about halfway through the afternoon, a time when he figured men would wait till the next morning before making any important moves. Unless, of course, some had already decided to head out to the North Fork.

It didn't seem so. The town was crowded, and he could feel the pulse of excitement the moment he rode in. He rode right to the livery to see if Willie was there, but it was only Eli, an old man who spoke maybe a half-dozen words a day, if that.

He rubbed down his pony, fed him, and gave the old hostler money. Then, on second thought, he saddled the horse again and left his bridle hanging around his neck.

Ten minutes later he had walked into the Buffalo Bar, where about all he could hear was the word "gold."

He had been standing at the bar only a few minutes, and had only taken one sip of his beer, when the bartender—Highpockets Purdy—told him Mr. Ratigan wanted to see him in his office down in the livery.

Slocum had heard that Ratigan had an office in the livery, but had always associated him with his office in the Buffalo Bar. He didn't leave immediately, but stayed with his beer, turning the situation over in his mind. He knew that if he didn't show up soon, Ratigan would send an escort. In fact, he wouldn't have been surprised to learn that the escort was already in the barroom with him. The situation smelled. At the same time, he knew he had to confront Ratigan sooner or later, and sooner was better. Except that it ought to be on Slocum's terms, and not the gambler's.

He took his time, turning it all over in his mind, trying to visualize the setup at the livery. When he saw in the mirror that someone was approaching him he put down his beer and left.

It was the end of the day, and it was relatively quiet outside after being in the Buffalo with everyone talking about gold. And it was the time of day he liked best. The sun was just about hitting the horizon and was throwing long golden rays over the town. He looked around him. Ratigan's town. And the man wanted more. Well, so far, the gambler was up on Miles as far as the Double R was concerned, though only on account of Slocum. Maybe that was what Ratigan wanted to see him about. Or maybe he'd gotten news of Sables.

He had almost arrived at the livery, and was just passing an alley, when he heard his name called. Turning his head he saw someone beckoning, and when he went over he found the young boy, Willie, who helped old Eli at the livery.

"They . . . they're l-layin' for you, Mr. S-Slo-cum."

"Thanks for letting me know, Willie. Who is there?"

"T-T-Tice an' Mister Ra-Ra-Ratigan. And t-two m-m-men."

"Four of them."

"Th-they know about S-S-Sables."

"That's a big help, Willie. I sure appreciate it." He turned to go, but the boy touched his arm.

"M-My s-s-sister s-s-sent this." And he handed Slocum something in a slicker.

It was a cut-down shotgun.

"Where in hell did you get this, Willie? And who's your sister?"

"G-Ginny. She s-s-said you could be c-carryin' a slicker, l-like f-for rain."

Suddenly a man passed them, and the boy drew back into the shadow of the alley. Slocum looked up at the sky. There were clouds, and it was almost nightfall. Yes, he could be carrying a slicker.

"Thank Ginny for me, Willie. And thank you, too."

But the boy was already turning away, perhaps exhausted from all the conversing, Slocum thought.

The front of the livery was deserted save for his own horse and some others. Eli, the hostler, was no-where around. Perhaps he had taken off when he'd seen what was up. Slocum walked down to the end of the big barn with the goose gun well covered by his slicker and his handgun ready for a fast draw.

The office was at the far end, and he saw the light. He walked quietly, without making a sound,

looking up at the loft above him and into the corners
and the stalls as he proceeded to the back of the big
structure.

He didn't knock. He simply walked in, still holding the slicker, loose, hanging down over his left
hand, like a kind of afterthought on the possibility of
rain.

Shiner Ratigan and Tice Finnegan sat at a round
table. There were cards in front of them, and drinks,
and the room was smoky from their cigars.

"Come in, Slocum. I've heard the news that
there's gold at the North Fork, and I've heard the
news that there isn't any gold at the North Fork."

"What did you want to see me about?" Slocum
asked, well aware that the two extra men that Willie
had mentioned were not in view.

"To offer you congratulations on, uh, the dis-
patching of Mr. Scarf Sables. Ably done, I was in-
formed."

"News travels fast on the frontier, don't it," Slocum said.

Tice said nothing during the exchange, only
looked steadily at Slocum.

"So what else?" Slocum said.

Shiner's eyebrows lifted in surprise. He opened
his hands, offering. "What else? Just my—our—
congratulations on a job well done."

"I see."

"You are free to go. I don't have any more need of
your services."

Slocum was standing well away from the door, a
habit he had learned early in his career, always to

move away from a door as soon as he entered through it.

Now he turned a little, so he could take the doorway into his line of vision. He saw Ratigan cut his eye at Tice Finnegan. And at that moment he dropped the slicker and pointed the scattergun at them.

"Either of you makes one sound, one move, and I'll cut the two of you right off at the knees."

Shiner's face had drained of color. Tice's lips tightened.

"Drop your guns onto the table," Slocum said, speaking softly in case anyone was listening. "Quick!"

"Slocum, what's the meaning of this? What are you doing? You can go, I don't need you anymore. This is crazy!"

"Now call those two knotheads in who're waiting to bushwhack me when I go out. I mean right now. But unbuckle first."

Both unbuckled their guns and laid them on the table.

"And the hideout," snapped Slocum.

Each had a belly gun.

"Now call them in. I already told you—right now."

Shiner Ratigan was staring at him with horror. Tice was staring with hatred. It was Shiner who lifted his voice.

"Otis, Sloane, come in here."

In a moment the two men entered.

"Drop 'em right on the floor. Quick," Slocum snapped.

"Slocum, what's the meaning of this? I thought we had an understanding, man."

"It means your little game with Lander Miles fell through, Ratigan."

"My game with Miles?"

"To take over the whole of the North Fork territory."

"You're crazy!"

"And you are dumb. You want to know something? You were easy to spot. You know how? You're just too damn sure of yourself. When you start thinking you're the Almighty it's the start of the end. Especially in your line of work."

"But how?" Shiner demanded. "I don't know what you're talking about."

"Oh yes you do. See, there really is gold up at the North Fork. But gold you planted there."

"You're lying!"

"I found some caught in my horse's shoe when I was out at the Double R."

"Shit!" Ratigan wheeled on Tice Finnegan, purple in the face. "You horse's ass, why weren't you more careful?"

"But he couldn't have caught it in his horse's shoe, Shiner. What kind of bullshit is that?" Tice said, glaring at Slocum.

"You're just guessing, Slocum," Shiner said. "I'll deny everything you say."

"You salted that gold out there so it could be found. You got that old man to ride in with his burro and his gold nugget. And you got Miles, who was hot for that rangeland, to help you without his knowing it. Then you put on an act about it being a fake. All innocent! Beautiful!"

"I'll deny everything you say, Slocum! Goddamn you!" Ratigan suddenly fell into an attack of coughing, which swiftly became a retching, as though he was choking. Otis stepped forward to help him, moving in front of Slocum.

In that instant, Ratigan made a grab for his gun, which was on the table, and Tice did likewise.

Both their shots went wild. Slocum, not using the shotgun in that close area, instead drew his .45 and shot Ratigan in the chest and Tice Finnegan right between the eyes.

Otis Dooley had turned white as a sheet. "Glory be to God!" he murmured, folding his terrified eyes into their lids.

Ratigan was only wounded, though not lightly. He would be out of action for a while. Tice Finnegan was out of the action forever. The game was ended.

Later, when he found Willie, Slocum asked him how come his sister had such a handsome cut-down 12-gauge.

"I-I told you she got it, b-but it was m-me."

"Where did you get it, Willie?"

"Th-that's Mr. R-Ratigan's. I g-g-got it out of his office."

And so, Slocum reflected, the bunco artist had been buncoed twice in one game. Good enough.

Later, paying his due respects to Ginny, he told her what a fine boy her brother was.

"I like him," she said simply, slipping down along his body as they lay naked together. "And I like you, too," she added.

"I like you, Ginny," Slocum said.

"Will you be around awhile? Or I guess that's a dumb thing to ask."

"I'll be around," he said.

"Then so will he," she said, holding his rigid penis in her fist.

The next morning he told her he would be away for a couple of days or so, and she smiled and said, "Whenever you want it, my friend."

That was the way Slocum liked it, and he told himself that the next day as he rode out of town toward the Double R. He knew he wasn't going to hang around there too long, but he surely ought to check up on things and see that young Brom was taking good care of those sisters. And maybe, if things went well—and he saw no reason why they shouldn't—maybe he could take some good care of the elder of the two, Nellie.

JAKE LOGAN
TODAY'S HOTTEST ACTION WESTERN!

__SLOCUM AND THE HANGING TREE #115	0-425-10935-6/$2.95
__SLOCUM AND THE ABILENE SWINDLE #116	0-425-10984-4/$2.95
__BLOOD AT THE CROSSING #117	0-425-11233-0/$2.95
__SLOCUM AND THE BUFFALO HUNTERS #118	0-425-11056-7/$2.95
__SLOCUM AND THE PREACHER'S DAUGHTER #119	0-425-11194-6/$2.95
__SLOCUM AND THE GUNFIGHTER'S RETURN #120	0-425-11265-9/$2.95
__THE RAWHIDE BREED #121	0-425-11314-0/$2.95
__GOLD FEVER #122	0-425-11398-1/$2.95
__DEATH TRAP #123	0-425-11541-0/$2.95
__SLOCUM AND THE TONG WARRIORS #125	0-425-11589-5/$2.95
__SLOCUM AND THE OUTLAW'S TRAIL #126	0-425-11618-2/$2.95
__SLOW DEATH #127	0-425-11649-2/$2.95
__SLOCUM AND THE PLAINS MASSACRE #128	0-425-11693-X/$2.95
__SLOCUM AND THE IDAHO BREAKOUT #129	0-425-11748-0/$2.95
__STALKER'S MOON #130	0-425-11785-5/$2.95
__MEXICAN SILVER #131	0-42511838-X/$2.95
__SLOCUM'S DEBT #132	0-425-11882-7/$2.95
__SLOCUM AND THE CATTLE WAR #133	0-425-11919-X/$2.95
__COLORADO KILLERS #134	0-425-11971-8/$2.95
